LITERARY OUTLAW

A PULP FICTION MAGAZINE | ISSUE #2

IN THIS ISSUE:

PRECIOUS IN THY SIGHT

BY KEVIN G. SUMMERS

HE DID IT IN SECRET, IN THE DARK hours of the night when nothing good ever happens. He did it in broad daylight, with the doors locked and the window shades drawn, whenever an opportunity presented itself. He would have been ashamed if his mother knew about this part of his life, but his mother was dust now and there was no one left to tell him that he was destroying himself. No one cared. It began as an impulse, but over time it evolved into an addiction, and eventually a fetish. It wasn't until he had driven everyone away, until the only thing that mattered was the behavior he thought of as his *Precious*, that John Galen realized he had a demon.

The first time he saw it was on a sweltering August night after a gig in Harlan, Kentucky. He was packing up his guitar and the rest of his equipment when a woman approached him from the crowd.

"Can I buy you a beer?" she asked.

She was wearing a plaid blouse that was just a little too short and a pair of Daisy Dukes that were just a little too tight. Her face was pretty enough and her body was about the best he could hope for in a town this size.

"Thank you," he said. "That would be wonderful."

She sauntered toward the bar like a cat, and Galen noticed the rose tattoo on her lower back—her tramp stamp. He took her back to his motel room and they fornicated with the lights off so Galen wouldn't have to look at her face. He thought her name was Candice, but he wasn't sure.

It was 2:22 a.m. when Galen awoke in the darkness. Candice lay beside him, sleeping soundly, and he wondered if she was the type that would sneak out at 6 a.m. or the kind that wanted to have breakfast and another roll in the sheets before she went back to whatever life she led here in this redneck town.

Galen felt like someone was watching him. He tried to tell himself that he was dreaming, but he couldn't shake the feeling no matter what he did. He turned slowly to a chair on the far side of the room and that's when he saw the demon sitting there, smiling in the darkness.

The sensation was uncanny, there was no other word for it. Galen was startled by the unexpected presence in the room and felt like jumping out of his skin, but he was paralyzed with fear. The figure in the chair seemed to be made of living shadow, and its eyes and mouth were nothing more than smudges of black on black, but Galen knew at once that it was looking at him and grinning horribly.

"Who are you? What do you want?"

He tried to speak but no words escaped his paralyzed lips. Still, the demon somehow understood his thoughts. It spoke in his mind, its voice low and terrible.

"Would it not feel good to put your hands around that whore's neck and choke the life out her?"

Galen was assaulted by the image of Candice's face as she struggled for breath. He tried to shake the thought away, but it was overwhelming.

"Kill her," said the demon. "Give her what she deserves."

Galen tried to resist, but no amount of willpower could overcome the demon who was rooted inside of him. He knew it was wrong to even think these thoughts, but he couldn't shake them. Candice's gasping face flashed on and off like a strobe light in the pleasure center of his brain, and slowly, very slowly, the notion of right and wrong faded. He wanted to hurt her because it made him feel good to think about hurting her.

He sat up in bed, rubbed his eyes, and took another look at the chair in the corner. The demon was still sitting there, watching voyeuristically at the scene unfolding before him. Galen knew there were demons in the world, but to see one and know that it dwelt inside of him like a parasite…that was a terrible thought. He had been a man of faith once upon a time, but that was long ago and far away. He had stood barefoot on the sacred ground of Israel and seen the places where Jesus walked upon the land, but it was so easy to turn your back on the Word. The demon smiled—its mouth like something out of a nightmare—and another wave of desire rippled through John Galen.

Hurt her.

Kill her.

Do it now.

Galen rolled on top of Candice and began kissing her face and neck. She stirred in her sleep as he rolled on top of her, and all the while he could hear the demon urging him on. It would be so easy to just tighten his grip and choke this poor woman to death. Galen wanted to do it, wanted that more than anything in the world. He reached for her throat.

"What are you doing?" Candice's voice was soft and sleepy.

"Nothing, I…"

"Get off me, I don't like that."

There was a moment when Galen hesitated, when all the power of the demon in his heart urged him to squeeze, but his sense of self-preservation was too strong. If he killed this woman he would be caught, that was a certainty, and he didn't want to go to jail. Galen rolled back to his side of the bed. He looked toward the chair in the corner of the room but the demon was gone.

"That's a creepy way to wake up," Candice said. "I know musicians can be into some freaky—"

"Get out."

"What?"

"You heard me, I said get out." Galen slipped out of bed, naked as Adam in the garden, and flipped on the light.

"Honey, I just didn't like…"

"It doesn't matter," Galen said, "you need to get out of here right now. I…I'm sorry. Just leave."

Candice threw the covers off and started gathering up her discarded clothing. It felt cruel to cast her out so suddenly, but the whole thing was just wrong and after he had come so close to murder, Galen knew he wouldn't be able to resist the demon a second time. He had to get the girl out of there and figure out what was happening to him.

"You're an asshole, you know that?" Candice was halfway into her clothes and she was steaming mad. "You think it's fun to choke a girl and then you get your panties in a wad when I tell you no? You're not much of a singer, even less of a guitar player, and you're about the worst lover I've ever had. You know that?"

The words stung, but Galen resisted the urge to lash out at her. She was right about all of it anyway. "Just get out of here," he said. "I'm sorry."

"Whatever, I hope you have a nice life, asshole."

She slammed the door on her way out and Galen was left alone in his motel room. He was thankful that he didn't have to spend the rest of the night trying to dispose of a dead body but that was a small consolation. He could feel the demon inside of him, twisting and gnawing in his brain like a maggot. He felt he might go mad if he thought about it too hard, and so he turned to his only comfort in the long, dark hours of the night—his *Precious*.

A year had passed and the demon had yet to resurface. Galen could still feel it inside of him, but he kept it at bay with every distraction under the sun. He drank too much, smoked too much, ate like a glutton, and binge-watched TV shows on Netflix. He snorted cocaine, and shot up with heroin, and downed countless prescription drugs which were easy enough to come by. He avoided women, terrified that whatever dwelt inside of him would seize control if he allowed himself to be intimate with a member of the fairer sex.

Galen was driving to a recording session in Nashville when he saw a flicker of movement in his rearview mirror. He looked closer and saw, to his horror, a woman sitting in the backseat…A woman who had been dead for ten years. He slammed on the brakes and his old Land Cruiser skidded to a stop in the middle of the road. The car behind him missed rear-ending him by inches, and the driver was blaring on the horn and flipping the bird as he drove around. Galen didn't care, he turned around in his seat to look at the woman who had been his lover once upon a time.

When he looked in her eyes he knew that this wasn't Lauren, but the demon wearing her skin.

"What's the matter, Darling…did you miss me?" It spoke with Lauren's voice, and the sound was like a dagger in Galen's heart. He was instantly transported back to the apartment he and Lauren shared a decade earlier in Fairfax, Virginia. They had known love and laughter in the two years they'd spent in each other's arms, and for a glimmer of time, he thought he had found a piece of happiness. But joy was fleeting and he ruined everything because he refused to give up his precious.

"You're not Lauren," Galen said. He took his foot off the break and touched the gas. The green Land Cruiser started rolling again down the highway toward Music City. He was in the suburb of Hendersonville, which was a bit of good luck considering he had just slammed on the brakes in the middle of a major road. If he had been in the city when he pulled that stunt he would have caused an accident for certain.

"I can be anyone you want me to be," said the demon. "Lauren…Shania Twain…your mother—"

"Stop. Please, why are you doing this to me?"

"I love you," said the demon, "and I want to give you what you want."

"I want you to go away," Galen said. "Get out of my head and leave me alone." He stole a glance at the monster in the rearview mirror. Lauren was sitting back there, smiling her terrible smile and staring at him with eyes that were cold and dead. He hated himself for what happened to her but there was nothing he could do about it now. Was there?

"You don't really mean that," said the demon wearing Lauren's skin. "Why don't you hit that school bus up there."

They were approaching an intersection, a four-way stop, and a big, yellow school bus was stopped to his right. The driver looked both ways, waited to be sure that no one was going to drive out of turn, and then rolled into the intersection.

Galen's foot shifted involuntarily on the brake. The Land Cruiser rolled forward an inch.

"Do it," said the demon. "Step on the gas and send those kids to meet Jesus. You'll walk away from the accident without even a scratch."

"Please," Galen said, "please, don't make me do this." His foot shifted again. He was trying to fight the monster in his head, but it was so, so difficult.

The demon didn't answer, only sat the in the back seat wearing Lauren's skin and watching him in the rearview mirror. Galen tried to resist, but the demon's suggestion overwhelmed him. He knew it was wrong, this thing the monster wanted him to do, but every neuron in his brain was firing, urging him to smash into the bus. The very thought of it, while revoltingly evil, gave him pleasure. He couldn't help himself.

Galen's foot went from the brake to the gas. He floored the pedal, and the Land Cruiser lurched away from the stop sign like a stock car at Daytona. The old truck's pick up was poor, and the engine strained as the automatic transmission climbed through the gears. It bore down on the school bus, and Galen was vaguely aware that the children inside were pointing at him and screaming in terror.

He knew he should pray, but the idea of speaking to God frightened John Galen. They didn't exactly have the best relationship these days, and the fact that he was carrying around a demon meant that God had abandoned him.

Didn't it?

The Land Cruiser missed by inches, and the bus stopped as soon as it passed through the intersection. Once the danger was passed, the pleasure center of Galen's brain shut down and absolute terror exploded inside of him. Whatever was inside of him, this demon, he couldn't control it. He had very nearly killed all those kids on the school bus, just as he had nearly killed that woman the year before. It was only a matter of time before his resistance slipped and he found himself with blood on his hands.

"Why are you doing this to me?" he shouted. He looked in the rearview mirror and saw that Lauren—the thing wearing Lauren's skin—was gone. He also noticed the flashing blue lights of a police cruiser in the rearview mirror.

Galen pulled off to the side of the road and the cop pulled up behind him. He thought about the recording session he had scheduled in Nashville in less than an hour, and he wondered if he was going to make it in time. Music was the one thing that let him forget his troubles for a little while—that and his *Precious*—but it seemed increasingly difficult to pick up his guitar and make the time. That didn't make any sense when he thought about it, because the music would just flow out of him as soon as he started strumming the chords, but just taking his guitar out of the case felt like the most difficult thing in the world sometimes.

The state trooper walked up beside the Land Cruiser and knocked on the window. Galen touched the button that lowered the glass and it disappeared inside the door.

"What in the blue hell were you doing back there?" asked the trooper. "Did you even see that bus?"

"Yes. I mean…no." Galen was a terrible liar, he knew it, and the demon wasn't back there now to help him get out of the situation. He felt his stomach twist into a knot.

"Either you did or you didn't," said the trooper. "Are you drunk?"

"No. No, sir. I…my foot slipped off the brake and I flew out into the intersection. I didn't mean to scare anyone. Is everyone ok?"

The trooper looked at him from behind a pair of mirrored sunglasses. When Galen saw his reflection in the glasses he noticed Lauren sitting in the passenger seat beside him. He turned to look at her and, sure enough, there she was. She smiled at him sweetly, keeping her mouth shut, and Galen had to force himself to remember that this wasn't really his old lover, but the demon that lived in his head.

"Call him a fascist pig," said the demon, "and spit on him."

Terror seized over Galen as he turned back to the officer. He tried to resist, but he heard the words come out of his mouth before he could control himself. He spat on the cop, and the next thing he knew he was being dragged from the car. Galen looked through the windshield as the state trooper bent him over the hood of his car and bound his hands behind his back. There was the demon, staring at him from the passenger seat and laughing like it was the funniest thing it had ever seen.

Galen wondered what was happening to him, where this demon came from, as he was being shoved into the back of the cruiser. Try as he might, he had no idea.

HE SPENT THE REST OF THAT DAY IN the Hendersonville Jail, in a tiny holding cell with a single bed and a barred window that looked out over a parking lot. He sat there on the bed, wondering if they had changed the sheets since the last time they held a prisoner in here, and trying to pray to a god whom he had ignored for a lifetime. The words didn't come easily.

"Why did you let this happen to me?" he said in the darkness.

"It wasn't God," said a familiar voice, "it was you."

Galen turned and saw Lauren lying on the bed beside him. She was naked and as beautiful as he remembered, and it was the most natural thing in the world for him to reach out and touch her. She was as cold as ice.

"Who are you?"

"I'm Lauren, your lover."

"No, Lauren is dead. Who are you really? What's your name?"

"My name is Legion, for we are many."

The words were familiar, but Galen couldn't place them. "What are you? Why are you following me?"

"I am an angel…your angel…and you chose me."

Galen had lived a long time in this world, and he had no memory of ever asking this supernatural creature to live in his head. "I don't understand," he said. "Where did you come from?"

Lauren sighed. "Are you sure you want to talk? There are other things we could do that might be a lot more… pleasurable." She touched him with her icy hand and Galen trembled in his soul. Her touch was both terrible and wonderful at the same time.

"Tell me," he pleaded. "I need to know."

"You found me online," said the demon. "You were looking at a certain website and there was a pop-up window. It said, 'Click yes and you'll never feel lonely again.' And you clicked yes."

Galen stared at her, incredulous. "I don't remember that."

"You were kind of distracted, but one little click and that's how you and me became we." Lauren smiled, revealing a mouth full of fangs. "You downloaded me through your eyes and into your brain, and now, here I am."

She ran her hands over her perfect body and Galen felt his resolve weaken. He reached for her again, and this time she was warm and soft. Lauren trembled under his hand as all sense of logic and rationality departed from Galen's mind. They fornicated in that little jail cell and it was wonderful and terrible at the same time. Afterward, they lay in each other's arms on the tiny bed.

"Why do you try to make me do horrible things?" Galen asked.

"Because I hate you," said Lauren. "What? Why?"

"I hate you as I hate all life, and your suffering gives me pleasure." She leaned close to him and whispered in his ear. "Do you know why I took the form of your former lover?"

Galen felt a knife stick into his heart. He had been happy for a time when Lauren Preston had been his girl, but he ruined everything, just like he always did. "Please, I don't…"

"Lauren Preston wanted nothing more than to be your bride," said the demon, "even though you waited and waited and never worked up the guts to ask her. She would have said, 'yes' in a heartbeat, did you know that?"

Galen tried to fight back tears.

"You made her do things that she hated. You degraded her and still she loved you because her heart was full of goodness. You poisoned that goodness until every bit of hope she carried was nothing but ashes, and then you screwed her sister in the very bed you shared with Lauren. Women don't just get over something like that."

The demon laughed and the sound was like a fist closing around Galen's heart. He hated himself for the things he had done. Even at the time it was happening, he knew he was doing wrong, but he couldn't control himself. It was like he was possessed.

"It was you," he said. "You made me do those things. You caused this."

The thing wearing Lauren's skin smiled its terrible smile. "You downloaded me and gave me a place to dwell," it said. "I like to think that we did it all together."

Galen cried out in desperate anger and grabbed the demon by the throat. He wasn't even aware that he was making a low, guttural sound in this throat like an animal. Lauren struggled beneath him as he tried to snuff the demon out of existence. He closed his eyes for just a second, and when he opened them again he had the bed sheet wrapped around his neck and was hanging from the bars of his cell. Deputies were swarming around him like bees—one was trying to hold him up, and another was trying to cut the sheet with a pocket knife. In that bleary state of near-death, he saw Lauren sitting on the bed, smiling at him.

"Lauren left your apartment after she found her sister in your arms. She went back home to the house where she grew up and hung herself in the closet where she used to keep her dress-ups. It was all your fault."

Galen tried to deny it, but he couldn't speak. Even if he could, he knew that it was the truth. He had opened his heart to this monster and had been unable to control the demon that raged inside of him. In pride and self-indulgence he had chosen a life of bondage to this demon, and for the life of him he could not see how to break free.

★ ★ ★

John Galen was transported to a mental health facility in Knoxville, Tennessee, where he spent the next three and a half years looking at Rorschach patterns and eating anti-psychotic drugs and talking to a string of therapists, all of whom were convinced that his problems were entirely chemical in nature. These were men and women of science, who believed that demons were no more real than Santa Claus or the Tooth Fairy. Galen gave up trying to convince them what was really happening to him, and, after a while, even he began to accept their explanations for what was going on. He swallowed their drugs and felt nothing. No one came to see him and the world outside forgot that he even existed.

He had no idea what became of his worldly possessions. He had his guitar because it was with him in the Land Cruiser on the day he was arrested, but everything else was lost to him. He didn't care about the clothes and furniture in his apartment—he had lived long enough to know that those were all replaceable—but he had a box of old photographs that was dear to him, and it broke his heart to think that he would never again be able to look at the faces of the people he had loved in earlier part of his life. As for the future, Galen held no hope whatsoever that he would ever be able to leave this facility. His life was over now, and there was nothing left for him to do but sit on his bed and wait for the Day of the Lord.

He sat.

He waited.

Sometimes he would hold his guitar and pick the beginning of a tune. His fingers did it mechanically, finding the notes and filling up the empty space with sound that bordered on being music. He never sang because singing comes out of a person's heart and the cocktail of medication he consumed twice daily had built a wall around his heart that was taller and more impenetrable than the one President Trump was building along the Mexican border. He watched the shift in presidential power without emotion. He saw men speak as if they were going to change the world, but Galen had seen it all before and he knew that whatever happened one day, whatever they did, someone else would come along and undo it in two years or four or eight.

It didn't matter.

Nothing mattered.

Time wore on.

The demon still came around sometimes, and whenever it did Galen would have another episode and the doctors would increase his medication. He couldn't even pronounce some of the drugs they had him on, and could hardly move when the thing wearing Lauren's skin climbed on top of him and rode him in the cold, dark night. He found a word somewhere, perhaps in one of the novels down in the mental facility's pathetic excuse for a library.

Succubus.

Was that what this thing was... this demon that dwelt inside of him? It assumed a female shape, but somehow Galen understood that it was neither male nor female by nature. He lay in its arms one night, exhausted but unable to sleep, when the demon spoke in the darkness.

"I'm going to leave you for a time," it said.

The thought terrified Galen. He pleaded with the demon for it to stay even though he knew that it was destroying him.

"Fear not, our separation will be brief. There's something I want you to do for me, and you can't do it in here." Lauren's mouth opened in a grin, revealing the terrible blackness that swirled just below the surface of her skin. Galen wanted to scream but he could not.

He began to make rapid improvements, and it wasn't long before the administrators of the mental health facility felt that he was ready to be released back into the wide world outside. It was a chilly spring morning when he walked out the hospital with nothing but the clothes on his back and his guitar slung over one shoulder like a troubadour. He had a wad of prescriptions in his pocket and no means of paying for the drugs that, supposedly, would keep the demon that lived inside of him at bay. He headed for the highway, shivering all over as the cold seeped into his bones. He doubted anyone reputable would pick him up, but he had to get as far away from Knoxville as possible, and since he had no means of transportation, he had to hitchhike.

A semi picked him up an hour later and he was rolling north and east, toward the glittering white city where the King of America sat on his marble throne.

★ ★ ★

"Do you know where you're going to go when you die?"

The trucker was an older man, in the autumn of his middle age, and he looked like he had lived hard. Galen didn't expect him to be a Bible thumper, not by the look of him, and at first he wondered if the demon inside of him had assumed a new form. The demon had been quiet these past few months, wanting him to be free of the sanitarium, but Galen always knew that it was in there, biding its time.

"I don't know," he admitted.

"Have you met Jesus?"

Galen smiled in spite of himself. "I have, though it's been a long time."

The trucker launched into a message of evangelism, and Galen was taken back to the dusty road outside of Jerusalem that led to a hill called Golgotha. It was written in the Gospels that the Son of Man had given his apostles the ability to cast out demons, but Galen was skeptical that any of his followers could still wield the Holy Spirit in this way. It was doubtful, but still, wasn't it worth trying? He had, literally, nothing to lose.

That's when he looked up and saw his reflection in the mirror on his side of the truck. The demon, still wearing the shape of his lost lover, was sitting next to him, in between Galen and the driver. She was smiling as if she had just heard a joke that she found hilarious.

Galen turned to look at her, and he knew in his heart that if she told him to reach across the seat and strangle the driver he would be unable to stop himself. His heart trembled as the demon leaned close to him and and whispered in his ear.

"This man is going to leave you in a suburb of the White City. Once there, you're going to sell your prescriptions and use the money to purchase a Glock. It's an impressive weapon, you'll like the way it feels in your hands when you use it."

"Please, don't make me hurt anyone," Galen said in his mind. It was no use trying to fight the demon that lived within him, he had been broken by its superior will long before. Still, he had to try.

"You're going to do more than hurt people. There's a school field trip headed into the White City in two day's time. Middle schoolers." The demon grinned wickedly. "You're going to sacrifice them in my name.

It was dusk when Galen arrived in the town of Carmel, Virginia. The trucker left him in a Wal-Mart parking lot, and for that Galen was deeply grateful. The demon in his head had been telling him for hours that he should cut the poor man's throat and leave him on the side of the road, but thus far Galen had been able to resist the temptation. He wasn't sure if he could have resisted for much longer.

Standing in the parking lot, Galen realized that he had nowhere to lay his head that night, and while it was spring, the nights were still cold and he didn't fancy the idea of sleeping out of doors. Carmel was a suburb of Washington, D.C., a bedroom community that had once been an important town when the world was larger and less connected.

He started walking.

It was a Saturday night in a populated area, and it wasn't long before Galen found a wayside bar. He had no money in his pocket, but he had his prescriptions and he figured they might be almost as good.

The bar was called the King's Court Tavern. It was dark and narrow and reeked of decades of cigarette smoke that could never be washed out of the old floorboards. The place was nearly empty, and no waitress offered to show him to his seat when Galen darkened the doorway. He approached the bar, found a spot next to the only other customer in the tavern, and sat down. The man had a day's worth of stubble on his cheeks and was hunched over his drink like it was something precious to him. He looked like Gollum, and the sudden image in Galen's mind was painful.

My Precious.

"Hey there," Galen said as he sat down beside the man. He looked up and saw Lauren standing behind the bar, wiping a glass with a dirty rag. She winked at him and Galen's blood went icy cold.

"Lay your prescriptions on the bar," Lauren said, "and I'll work out the rest."

Galen closed his eyes and tried to resist, but he could not. This creature of pure evil lived inside of him—he had been foolish enough to invite her in—and he was powerless to resist whatever twisted command it uttered. He reached into his pocket and removed the prescriptions. He set three slightly crumpled pieces of paper on the glossy wood, and after a few moments, the man turned his head to look.

"How much do you want for those?" he asked.

Galen's eyes went to Lauren. "Tell him five hundred," she said.

"Five hundred dollars," said Galen.

The man stared at him for a long moment, sighed, and then reached for his wallet. He produced ten crisp fifty dollar bills and laid them on the bar. Galen took the money, counted it, and shoved it into the pocket where the prescriptions had been. The man grabbed the papers, slid off his bar stool, and was headed for the door all in the space of a few seconds. The transaction was done, and Galen was left sitting alone in the King's Court Tavern. It was like the whole thing had been set up for him, and maybe it had. If that man also had a demon in him, and by the look of him Galen thought that was likely, then perhaps the preternatural creatures had some way of communicating with one another. The thought was terrifying.

It wasn't long before an actual bartender appeared and apologized profusely that Galen had to wait for service. He pulled a beer from a tap behind the bar and served him the best fish and chips the wandering man had eaten in many a year. The fish was hot and crispy and the beer went down smooth. Galen thought of Jesus again, dining on his last supper with fools that hadn't understood a word he had said in three years. Jesus must have known what was coming—that a terrible death was waiting for him just up the road a ways—but there was nothing for him to do but eat his bread and drink his wine. For Galen, he understood that he would be powerless to stop this horror the demon wanted him to commit, and he was terribly sorry for what he was about to do.

THERE WAS A CONSTRUCTION SITE A block away from the tavern, and Galen found the building unlocked that Saturday night. This place had been a cinema once upon a time, but a fire had gutted the old building leaving a blackened ruin. The new theater they were building on the site looked magnificent, and Galen wished he could see the finished product, but he doubted that he would ever come this way again. It was cold that night, but at least he was dry, and no one bothered Galen as he slept. He decided in the night that he would make one final effort to defy the demon that lived inside of him. He knew that the chances were slim, but he had to try. Resisting evil was the duty of every man, and Galen hoped— prayed—that there was someone in this town that could deliver him from his burden.

He awoke the next morning, grimy from a day of hard travel and a night of hard drinking. In a word, John Galen was unclean. He thought about the long chain of mistakes he had made that had brought him to this point and hoped that today he would meet the one the one man who could break that chain.

Galen slipped out of the theater and walked along the sidewalks in the slumbering town of Carmel, Virginia. He had seen a beautiful church on the way into town, and it wasn't hard for him to backtrack the route and find the place again. The building glittered in the light of the morning sun—it appeared almost golden in that light, and Galen wondered if the people that worshipped here ever noticed the beauty of the Lord's house as they scrambled for a parking space, hoping that the minister wouldn't go overtime and cause them to miss the football game.

An elaborate sign stood at the corner of the property. It read:

> Carmel Bible Church
> Rev. Dr. Van Gernhardt
> Services: Saturday 4:00 p.m.
> Sundays 9:00, 10:30, 12:00

Galen crossed the parking lot, in the cold morning air. There were only a handful of cars, and the wandering man suspected that these might belong to some deacons or even the Reverend Dr. Gernhardt. His heart swelled with hope and anticipation as he drew near to God's house—this was the answer to his problem, he was certain. All he had to do was find this minister and ask him to cast out the demon in Jesus's name.

He reached the glass front doors of the church and found, to his amazement, that they were locked. Galen pressed his face to the thick glass and saw men in suits moving about the sanctuary. A heavyset man was standing at the pulpit and fiddling with a microphone. He could see them as plain as day, and unless this glass was tinted, Galen figured that they could probably see him as well, but they didn't look at him. He balled his right hand into a fist and rapped once on the glass door.

The men in the sanctuary turned to look at him; the reverend stared at him from the pulpit with a look of annoyance on his stern face.

"They won't be able to help you," said a familiar voice.

Galen's eyes went from the people inside the sanctuary to the demon, who stood beside him in front of the church. Lauren's lips parted in a grin, revealing the needle-sharp teeth of the demon beneath her skin.

"You don't know that," Galen said. "I'll tell them what you've done to me and they'll cast you out. That's how the story of Legion ends, don't you know?"

Lauren laughed. "Look for Jesus all you want," she said, "but you won't find him here."

Galen rapped on the door again, this time a little harder, and one of the deacons headed for the door. He was wearing a dark suit with a red tie, and his face was hard. He reached the door, turned the bolt lock, and opened the glass just a crack.

"Worship isn't for another hour," he said. He closed the door and bolted it again.

The demon was holding its belly and laughing so hard that it had to sit down. Galen banged on the door again, hard enough this time that he thought the glass might shatter. The deacon, who was halfway back to the pulpit, returned to the door and opened it again. This time, the expression on his face was clearly anger.

"I told you, we're not open yet..."

"Please," Galen said, "I need your help."

The deacon looked skeptical.

"There's something wrong with me…something in my head. I think it's a demon, and you all can cast out demons, right? Please, I need your help."

The deacon rolled his eyes and sighed. "Van," he said, "this guy says he has a demon and he wants you to exorcise him."

The reverend laughed. Galen was able to hear because the sound was projected into the sanctuary speakers through the microphone he wore.

"Demons aren't real," said Dr. Gernhardt, "you know that, Ed. Tell him to pound sand."

Galen fell to his knees, desperate that his last chance at redemption not slip through his fingers. "Please…I need Jesus. He can save me…deliver me from this abomination. I need your help."

The deacon whose name was Ed closed the glass door in Galen's face and turned the lock. Tears fell from the wandering man's eyes and splashed upon the white concrete step in front of Carmel Bible Church. He had come here in search of a miracle, but it was clear to him now that Jesus wasn't here. Hope was gone, and all that remained was the demon wearing Lauren's skin. The creature stood, brushed itself off, and helped Galen to his feet.

"Come on," it said, "I know a place where you can get that gun."

★ ★ ★

HE STUMBLED ALONG THE HISTORIC streets of Carmel, past Victorian homes that had stood for a century, and hipster shops that would be gone in a year. He passed through the nice suburbs, full of expensive McMansions that weren't quite as nice as the homes in the older part of town. He passed through middle class suburbs packed with durable houses that were built before the turn of the new millennium. And finally he came to the poor part of town, where obese children stared at him as he walked by. Galen felt a smoldering anger in his heart, and the demon that walked beside him was fanning the flames.

"Going to church didn't work out so well for you," it said. "Would you like to try another denomination or three before you admit that God has turned his back on you?"

The monster's words were like a slap in the face. Galen had been a man of faith once upon a time, but that was long ago and far away. He tried to pray every once in a while, but he was out of practice and the words did not come easily to him. The idea of bowing to anyone, even a god, was difficult for him, and he was beginning to accept the fact that God did not love him any more.

"It's so much worse than that," said the demon. "Not only does God not love you, he hates you. He wants to see you suffer."

"No…"

"Yes, you are cursed, that's why the followers of the Son of Man refused to even let you into his house. You are cursed, John Galen, and your soul belongs to no one but me."

Those words were poison for a man such a he, and the burden Galen carried grew heavier with every step. He had fallen so far from the person he wanted to be, fallen like lighting from Heaven, and Galen despaired in his heart. He was contemplating jumping in front of the next car that drove by when they stopped suddenly in front of a dilapidated house.

"This is the place," said the demon. "Go knock on the door and ask for Bray."

Galen obeyed without hesitation. He had managed to resist the creature in his head at the start of their relationship, but he knew now that all of his strength had gone. He knocked on the door and a pale woman appeared a few moments later. She was dark-eyed and wary, but she let Galen into the house as if she was expecting him. He stood in a cramped living room—the house had nothing so grand as a foyer—and waited until a heavyset man appeared from upstairs. He had long hair tucked under a baseball cap, and a beard that flowed down his chest like a wizard or a Pharasee. When Galen looked into Bray's eyes he saw nothing…no emotion whatsoever.

"How can I help you?" he asked.

"I need a gun," said Galen. "Maybe a Glock if you have one."

Bray's face betrayed no emotion as he spoke. "I have one. You've got five hundred?"

"I've got about four seventy-five." He spent the rest on supper and drinks the night before, and a small part of Galen hoped that the man would refuse the price.

He did not.

They made the deal and Galen left the house with a pistol tucked into his belt and a half dozen clips of ammunition—enough to kill seventy people if his aim was true. Somehow, he knew that it would be.

★ ★ ★

HE HAD SPENT EVERY DOLLAR IN HIS pocket, and so Galen was once again forced to use his thumb to catch a ride. He moved ever eastward, spending the rest of that Sunday creeping from suburb to suburb. He was hungry and cold and burdened by thoughts of what he was about to do. He knew it was wrong, but he couldn't help himself anymore. And in the midst of everything else, his thoughts turned ever to his *Precious*. When this was all done, when the bodies of three score school children were scattered all around him, Galen wondered if the demon would let him delve into the *Precious* once again.

Galen spent that night in an alley in Washington, D.C., the white city that claimed to be the capital of the world. It wasn't the first to make such a claim, and he wondered how long it would be before Washington went the

way of London and Rome and Babylon and Thera. It was only a matter of time.

He was starving when he awoke the next morning, but without any money he had no way to eat. He still had his guitar, and while he had sung for his supper many times, he had never heard of anyone singing for their breakfast.

The memory of a little compartment in the guitar case hit him like a ton of bricks. It was designed to hold picks and his capo, neither of which had seen much use these past few years, but Galen often kept some cash secreted away in that compartment as well—rainy day money for situations just like this one. He set the case on the ground and opened the latches one by one. The lid lifted up on its hinges, revealing the 1968 Gibson J50 that was his only possession in the world. It was a beautiful instrument, a classic that held its tune no matter how much or how little he played it. His fingers hovered over the strings, longing to bring their sweet sounds to life, but he resisted. Instead he lifted up the guitar and opened the compartment under its neck. There was a twenty dollar bill folded up inside. Galen removed the twenty, stuffed it into his pocket, and was setting the guitar back in its place when a voice spoke up behind him.

"That's a beauty, Mister. Can you play that thing?"

Galen turned to see a shabby-looking man standing in the alley behind him. His clothes were threadbare and he wore no shoes in spite of the cold morning. He was thin to the point of starvation and his eyes were set deep in his their sockets. He seemed familiar somehow, but Galen couldn't place him.

"I used to play," he said. "Now I just carry it around. A reminder, I suppose, of my old life."

"Have you got any change?" asked the stranger. He held out a styrofoam cup and gave it a little shake.

Galen thought about the twenty in his pocket. He was hungry, but this man clearly was as well. It was nothing, a token gesture, but the idea of doing a kindness to a stranger pleased him somehow. He fished the folded bill from his pocket and dropped it in the man's cup."

The homeless man smiled. "I'd love to hear you play. You could spare a minute to pick something for me, couldn't you?"

Galen thought about the ache in his belly and the weight of the gun tucked into his belt. Every step carried him closer to an act of terrible evil and he was in no hurry. He reached into the case and lifted out the guitar. He slid the strap over his shoulder, formed the C chord with his left hand, and strummed the strings one time to see if it was in tune. The sound was as sweet as honey.

"What do you want to hear?"

The homeless man smiled. "Oh, anything."

Galen closed his eyes and scanned through the musical library that was locked away in his head. He knew hundreds of songs, but he was having a difficult time dredging one up out of his memory. He had hardly played a note since his demon surfaced, and there had been a time when his music

was more precious to him than anything else.

Precious.

The wandering man formed a few chords and then began to pick a slow tune on the old Gibson. He closed his eyes as he slipped deeper into the song, and after a few moments, he began to sing.

Precious Lord, take my hand, lead me on, let me stand…

I'm tired, I'm weak, I'm alone.

Through the storm, through the night, Lead me on to the light…

Take my hand, Precious Lord, lead me home.

There were tears in Galen's eyes as he looked up at the stranger, and suddenly he recognized him. *He knew this man.* Galen was about to speak when the demon inside of him came up screaming to the surface of his mind.

He cried out and fell to his knees before the homeless man, and with a loud voice said, "What have I to do with you, Jesus, Son of the Most High God?"

The stranger just stared at him, his eyes deep pools of terrible sorrow. "Come out of him," he said in a calm, quiet voice that was almost a whisper.

Galen coughed violently, and from his mouth poured an oily, black smoke that took shape beside him in the alley. The demon that had tormented him no longer wore the skin of his former lover like a mask, but seemed instead to be made of living shadow. It stared at him for a moment, and Galen saw no anger or hatred in the creature's empty eyes, but only fear.

"I beg you," said the demon, "do not torment me."

The homeless man asked him, saying "What is your name?"

"My name is Legion," said the demon, "for we are many."

"Your true name…" said the man, Jesus.

The demon uttered something guttural, unpronounceable, and then broke into a fit of whimpering sobs. The creature was terrified.

The homeless man reached across the empty gulf between them and touched the shadowy demon. The monster screamed in agony as its body burned away like fog in the sunshine. The stranger who wasn't a stranger turned to look at Galen. He smiled. "That was some nice singing," he said. "You should do more gospel songs."

Still on his knees in the cold alley, Galen struggled to find his words. "I…I'm sorry," he said at last.

"I forgive you."

Galen thought of the bitter trial that had been his long life. He had invited the demon into his heart and mind, and had sinned continually since the day he was born. He thought about the last time he had seen this Son of Man, and the curse that had hung around his neck like an albatross. Surely, Jesus could not forgive him for all of that.

"I can," said the stranger, as if he had heard Galen's thoughts. "I can and I do, but you still must reap what you have sown."

Still weeping, still overwhelmed that he was free from the demon that had plagued him, Galen slid his guitar onto his back and bowed before his savior. When he looked up, the homeless man was gone.

★ ★ ★

JOHN GALEN THREW THE GUN INTO the Potomac River and thanked the Son of Man that things had not ended up differently. He was free at last, and though he was tempted even now, he vowed that he would never again return to the thing he did in secret… the thing that had invited a demon into his mind. The gun was a physical object, something he could touch, but in his heart Galen was tossing his *Precious* into the wide river below.

He crossed the bridge into Virginia on foot, and began a slow trek westward that afternoon, hitching his way from town to town, picking tunes in bars and restaurants and little wayside honky-tonks to pay his way. He wandered the nation and the world, for such was his burden, and sometimes, when he rode in the back of a pickup with the wind whipping through his hair or when he played an A.P. Carter song that no one had heard for decades, the wandering man smiled and thought that his burden wasn't so heavy after all.

THE END

the GHOST RIDER

THIS IS THE TALE OF THE GHOST RIDER —

A MAN BORN TO THE WEST! A MAN WHO HATES EVIL AND THE DEATHS AND ROBBERIES AND LOOTINGS THAT THE BANDITS AND OUTLAWS OF THE OLD WEST LEFT IN THEIR RUTHLESS PATH! A MAN TRAINED BY THE GHOSTLY HANDS OF THE MEN WHO MADE THE WEST SAFE, AND WHO GAVE THEIR OWN LIVES THAT OTHER MEN MIGHT LIVE!

WILD BILL HICKOK... PAT GARRETT WHO KILLED BILLY THE KID... CALAMITY JANE... KIT CARSON, WHO KNEW THE INDIANS AND THEIR WAYS ...

THIS, THEN, IS THE STORY OF HOW THE GHOST RIDER WAS BORN AND GREW, UNTIL THE LEGENDS OF HIM IN THE NIGHTS AROUND THE LONELY CAMP-FIRES SWEPT LIKE A COLD BREEZE DOWN THE SPINES OF THOSE WHO FEARED THE LAW...

DICK AYERS

IT ALL BEGAN WHEN A BAND OF APACHES, LED BY A WHITE MAN DISGUISED AS AN INDIAN, RAIDED THE LITTLE TRAVELLING STORE RUN BY A MAN NAMED REX FURY AND KNOWN AS "THE CALICO KID"...

LOOKS BAD, SING SONG!

THEY HAVE US SURROUNDED! ONE MORE CHARGE AND THEY'LL RUN RIGHT OVER US....!

ALTHOUGH REX FURY FOUGHT LIKE A MAN DEMENTED, THE APACHES PROVED TOO MUCH FOR HIM ...
I'LL TAKE PLENTY OF YOU WITH ME... WHEN I GO...!
KILL! KILL!

YOU! BART LASHER! A WHITE MAN — A RENEGADE KILLER!
YOU KNOW TOO MUCH, FURY! ESPECIALLY FOR A U.S. MARSHAL!

TAKE THIS HOMBRE TO THE DEVIL'S SINK!
OHHH!

LESS THAN AN HOUR LATER, IN THE ROCK HILLS OF THE BADLANDS, REX FURY AND SING SONG ARE FLUNG INTO THE ROARING WHIRLPOOL OF THE DEVIL'S SINK! NO MAN HAS EVER EMERGED ALIVE FROM ITS WATERY GRASP!

DEEPER AND DEEPER IN THE VORACIOUS WATERS SPIN THE TWO MEN... DRAGGED ALONG BY THE MAD CURRENT... BATTERED ON ROCKS... LUNGS BURSTING FOR AIR... UNTIL SUDDENLY THE WATERS RELEASE THEIR GREEDY GRIP...
GOT TO... REACH THAT ROCK LEDGE... REST.. REST AND AIR ... FOR MY LUNGS .....

FACE DOWN, REX FURY LIES AS ONE DEAD. HE DOES NOT SEE A GLOWING NIMBUS OF LIGHT, OR THE MAN WHO STEPS OUT OF IT...
HE IS FAR GONE... ALMOST DEAD! HE IS ON THE VERY BORDERLINE BETWEEN LIFE ... AND DEATH..!
REX FURY! AWAKE! OPEN YOUR EYES...
HUH? WHAT...? SAY... I KNOW YOU. YOU'RE WILD BILL HICKOK! BUT — YOU'RE DEAD! DEAD!

IT CAN'T BE! I'M DREAMING! YOU WERE SHOT IN 1876 BY JACK McCALL! YOU'RE DEAD!
WHAT MAKES YOU THINK YOU'RE ALIVE, REX FURY? YOU ARE ON THE VERY BORDERLAND... WHERE LIFE AND DEATH WALK FREELY. THAT IS WHY I CAN COME TO YOU...

BUT COME, WE MUST HURRY! THEY ARE ALL WAITING TO SEE YOU! WE HAVE SO LITTLE TIME...
"THEY?" WHO ARE THEY? WHERE ARE WE GOING?

PAT GARRETT, WHO SHOT BILLY THE KID! KIT CARSON, WHO FOUGHT THE INDIANS! CALAMITY JANE! OTHERS... ALL WAITING FOR YOU!
BUT I— I DON'T UNDERSTAND....

MANY OF THE MEN AND WOMEN WHO TRIED TO MAKE THE WEST SAFE FOR THE HOME-MAKERS ARE DEAD. BUT BANDITRY AND OUTLAWRY STILL FLOURISH! WE WANT TO HELP IN THE ONLY WAY WE CAN — BY PASSING ON OUR KNOWLEDGE TO ONE WHO CAN DO WHAT WE CANNOT...

LOOK THERE! TWO OLD FRIENDS — PROSPECTORS! THEY HAVE FOUND TRACES OF GOLD. NOW THEIR LIFELONG FRIENDSHIP IS FORGOTTEN. NOW ONE WILL TRY TO KILL THE OTHER ... AND WE CANNOT STOP IT! BUT A MAN LIKE YOU COULD... WITH OUR KNOWLEDGE!

SWIFTLY, WILD BILL HICKOK AND REX FURY MOVE ACROSS THE PLAINS, UNTIL THEY COME TO A STRANGE, UNREAL LAND, WHERE GHOSTLY RIDERS REIN THEIR HORSES TO A HALT BEFORE THEM...
PAT GARRETT! KIT CARSON!

CALAMITY JANE! BILLY TILGHMAN, MARSHAL OF DODGE CITY!
WELCOME TO THE OTHER WORLD, REX FURY! WE HAVE MUCH WORK TO DO. LET'S START....!

THE FIRST LESSON — WITH SIXGUNS — IS TAUGHT BY A MASTER OF THE TRADE — WILD BILL HICKOK !
WHEN YOU CAN DRIVE THE CORK INTO A BOTTLE AT FIFTY PACES, YOU'LL BE GOOD, REX — YOU'LL BE A MARKSMAN ...
PLICK!

PRACTICE ! CONSTANT PRACTICE ! ALWAYS KEEP AT IT, AND YOU'LL NEVER MISS ! ... THAT'S IT ... A FIRM GRIP .. EYES FIXED ON YOUR TARGET ! A GENTLE RELEASE OF THE HAMMER .. WRISTS SET FOR THE RECOIL ...

FOR SPEED OF DRAW — BILLY TILGHMAN !
I STOOD IN FRONT OF A BIG MIRROR HOUR AFTER HOUR ! I WATCHED MYSELF AS MY HANDS DREW OUT MY GUNS ... CUT OUT EVERY UNNECESSARY MOVE ! KEPT MY EYES COLD ... NEVER REVEALING THE MOMENT WHEN I WOULD GO FOR MY COLTS ...

HOUR BY HOUR, REX FURY'S HANDS GATHER THE MAGICAL SPEED AND ACCURACY OF THE GUNHANDS OF WILD BILL HICKOK AND BILLY TILGHMAN ...
HE'LL DO !
BETTER THAN ANY MAN ALIVE !

RIDING THE PRAIRIE WITH CALAMITY JANE ... LEARNING THE FINER POINTS OF RIFLE FIRE ...
KEEP YOUR MUZZLE STEADY ... WATCH THE SHADOWS MOVE ALONG YOUR BARREL WHEN YOU HAVE NO TIME TO LINE UP YOUR SIGHTS ...

AND THEN KIT CARSON TAKES REX FURY UNDER HIS WING
YOU HAVE TO LEARN TO HIDE YOUR TRACKS .. INJUNS CAN SEE A BLADE OF GRASS THAT'S BEEN MISPLACED ...

IT WON'T DO YOU ANY HARM TO LEARN HOW TO HEAVE A KNIFE. THERE'S MANY A TIME WHEN A PROPERLY THROWN KNIFE — SILENT AND DEADLY — CAN ACCOMPLISH WHAT A SIXGUN CAN'T !
THUD!

DON'T LAUGH AT AN INDIAN BOW AND ARROW, EITHER. THEY MAKE MIGHTY FINE WEAPONS! I'VE SEEN INJUN BUCKS DRIVE AN ARROW PLUMB THROUGH A BUFFALO!
SWIFTLY THE SKILL OF A MOUNTAIN MAN CAME TO REX FURY. SOON HE COULD RISE FROM A MOTIONLESS BRUSH, TOMAHAWK FLASHING AS HIS PRACTICED HAND THREW IT WITH DEADLY ACCURACY...
ONE THING YET REMAINS! YOU MUST HAVE A HORSE — A STREAK OF SWIFTNESS TO CARRY YOU ACROSS THE TRACKLESS PLAINS...
WHERE WILL I FIND SUCH A HORSE?
THERE, REX FURY! LOOK THERE!
I SEE HIM! I SEE HIM! A SILVER STALLION! A GIANT— WITH THE SPEED OF THE WIND!
FOR ENDLESS DAYS, IT SEEMS TO REX FURY, HE RIDES HORSE AFTER HORSE TO EXHAUSTED STAGGERS UNDER HIM, TRYING TO OVERTAKE THAT MIGHTY STALLION. AND THEN ONE DAY, WITH A LUCKY TOSS...
I CAN NEVER CATCH HIM ...NEVER! AND YET,... I MUST! MY ROPE... FALLING AROUND HIS NECK! I'VE GOT HIM!
WILD BILL HANDS REX FURY CLOTHES AND A HAT, AND A MASK TO COVER HIS FACE. AND SO, FOR THE FIRST TIME, THE GHOST RIDER COMES TO LIFE...
GOOD LUCK, GHOST RIDER!
USE YOUR NEW TALENTS WELL!
SOME HOURS AFTER SUNSET, THE GHOST RIDER COMES UPON A LONELY CAMPFIRE...
THE SKULKIN' COYOTE! HE'S FIXIN' TO SHOOT ME IN THE BACK!
HE'S GOIN' TO KILL ME. RECKON I'D BETTER KILL HIM FIRST!

LIKE A CLANGING BELL, THE CLEAR TONES OF THE GHOST RIDER SOUND ON THE NIGHT AIR!
SONS OF EVIL! WOULD-BE MURDERERS! STOP! DROP THOSE GUNS!
YOU WOULD KILL EACH OTHER FOR GOLD THAT IS NOT GOLD?
HUH? NOT GOLD?
WE FOUND IT TWO WEEKS AGO!
LOOK THERE! YOUR GOLD IN THE EMBERS OF YOUR CAMPFIRE! IT TURNS BLACK! IT IS NOT GOLD— BUT IRON PYRITES!
THUNDERATION! IRON PYRITES! THAT'S FOOL'S GOLD!
FORGIVE ME, PETE! I WAS A SUSPICIOUS OLD IDJIT!
YOU FORGIVE ME, TOO, ED! I RECKON WE'VE DONE LEARNED OUR LESSON!
AND, A LITTLE LATER, WITH DAZED SENSES AND WHIRLING BRAIN, REX FURY FINDS HIMSELF STAGGERING UP OUT OF A DEEP SLUMBER...
THAT'S US, ED—A COUPLE OF FOOLS!
NOW TO RETURN TO THE CAVE— AND SING SONG!
DID I DREAM ALL THAT? OR DID IT REALLY HAPPEN? I MUST KNOW! I MUST LEARN THE ANSWER....!
FOLLOWING THE SECRET PATH BESIDE THE UNDERGROUND RIVER WHICH HE LEARNED FROM WILD BILL HICKOK, REX FURY SOON FINDS HIMSELF OUTSIDE THE CAVE.. WHERE A GREAT STALLION SEEMS TO BE WAITING FOR HIM..
SPECTRE! ALIVE! YOU'RE NO DREAM, AT ANY RATE! AND I CAN MAKE THE COSTUME THAT THE GHOST RIDER IS TO WEAR AND TAKE UP THE CAUSE OF LAW AGAINST THE EVILDOERS WHO SEEK ONLY TO KILL AND ROB...
THUS CAME THE GHOST RIDER TO HAUNT THE TRAILS FROM TEXAS TO MONTANA, FROM MISSOURI TO KANSAS. HIS STATURE GREW WITH EVERY TALE OF HIM, UNTIL EVEN HARDENED CRIMINALS SHOOK WHEN RUMOR SAID HE WAS RIDING THE MIDNIGHT WINDS..
FASTER, SPECTRE, FASTER! THERE'S WORK TO BE DONE TONIGHT, BEFORE THE SUN COMES UP....!

DAGON
BY H. P. LOVECRAFT

I am writing this under an appreciable mental strain, since by tonight I shall be no more. Penniless, and at the end of my supply of the drug which alone makes life endurable, I can bear the torture no longer; and shall cast myself from this garret window into the squalid street below. Do not think from my slavery to morphine that I am a weakling or a degenerate. When you have read these hastily scrawled pages you may guess, though never fully realize, why it is that I must have forgetfulness or death.

It was in one of the most open and least frequented parts of the Pacific that the packet of which I was supercargo fell a victim to the German sea-raider. The great war was then at its very beginning, and the enemy's navy had not reached its later degree of ruthlessness, so that our vessel was made a legitimate prize, whilst we of her crew were treated with all the fairness and consideration due us as naval prisoners. So liberal, indeed, was the discipline of our captors, that five days after we were taken I managed to escape alone in a small boat with water and provisions for a good length of time.

When I finally found myself adrift and free, I had but little idea of my surroundings. Never a competent navigator, I could only guess vaguely by the sun and stars that I was somewhat south of the equator. Of the longitude I knew nothing, and no island or coast-line was in sight. The weather kept fair, and for uncounted days I drifted aimlessly beneath the scorching sun; waiting either for some passing ship, or to be cast on the shores of some habitable land. But neither ship nor land appeared, and I began to despair.

The change happened whilst I slept. Its details I shall never know; for my slumber, though troubled and dream-infested, was continuous. When at last I awaked, it was to discover myself half sucked into a slimy expanse of hellish black mire which extended about me in monotonous undulations as far as I could see, and in which my boat lay grounded some distance away.

Though one might well imagine that my first sensation would be of wonder at so prodigious and unexpected a transformation of scenery, I was in reality more horrified than astonished, for there was in the air and in the rotting soil a sinister quality which chilled me to the very core. The region was putrid with the carcasses of decaying fish, and of other less describable things which I saw protruding from the nasty mud of the unending plain.

The sun was blazing down from a sky which seemed to me almost black in its cloudless cruelty; as though reflecting the inky marsh beneath my

feet. As I crawled into the stranded boat I realized that only one theory could explain my position. Through some unprecedented volcanic upheaval, a portion of the ocean floor must have been thrown to the surface, exposing regions which for innumerable millions of years had lain hidden under unfathomable watery depths. So great was the extent of the new land which had risen under me, that I could not detect the faintest noise of the surging ocean, strain my ears as I might. For several hours I sat thinking or brooding in the boat, which lay upon its side and afforded a slight shade as the sun moved across the heavens. As the day progressed, the ground lost some of its stickiness, and seemed likely to dry sufficiently for traveling purposes in a short time. That night I slept but little, and the next day I made for myself a pack containing food and water, preparatory to an overland journey in search of the vanished sea and possible rescue.

On the third morning I found the soil dry enough to walk upon with ease. The odor of the fish was maddening; but I was too much concerned with graver things to mind so slight an evil, and set out boldly for an unknown goal. All day I forged steadily westward, guided by a far-away hummock which rose higher than any other elevation on the rolling desert. That night I camped, and on the following day still traveled toward the hummock, though that object seemed scarcely nearer than when I had first spied it. By the fourth evening I attained the base of the mound, which turned out to be much higher than it had appeared from a distance.

I do not know why my dreams were so wild that night, but before the waning and fantastically gibbous moon had risen far above the eastern plain, I was awake in a cold perspiration, determined to sleep no more. Such visions as I had experienced were too much for me to endure again. And in the glow of the moon I saw how unwise I had been to travel by day. Without the glare of the parching sun, my journey would have cost me less energy; indeed, I now felt quite able to perform the ascent which had deterred me at sunset. Picking up my pack, I started for the crest of the eminence.

I HAVE SAID THAT THE UNBROKEN monotony of the rolling plain was a source of vague horror to me; but I think my horror was greater when I gained the summit of the mound and looked down the other side into an immeasurable pit or canyon, whose black recesses the moon had not yet soared high enough to illumine. I felt myself on the edge of the world; peering over the rim into a fathomless chaos of eternal night. Through my terror ran curious reminiscences of Paradise Lost, and of Satan's hideous climb through the unfashioned realms of darkness.

As the moon climbed higher in the sky, I began to see that the slopes of the valley were not quite so perpendicular as I had imagined. Ledges and outcroppings of rock afforded fairly easy footholds for a descent, whilst after a drop of a few hundred feet, the declivity became very gradual. Urged on by an impulse which I cannot definitely analyze, I scrambled with difficulty down the rocks and stood on the gentler slope beneath, gazing into the Stygian deeps where no light had yet penetrated.

All at once my attention was captured by a vast and singular object on the opposite slope, which rose steeply about a hundred yards ahead of me; an object that gleamed whitely in the newly bestowed rays of the ascending moon. That it was merely a gigantic piece of stone, I soon assured myself; but I was conscious of a distinct impression that its contour and position were not altogether the work of Nature. A closer scrutiny filled me with sensations I cannot express; for despite its enormous magnitude, and its location in an abyss which had yawned at the bottom of the sea since the world was young, I perceived beyond a doubt that the strange object was a well-shaped monolith whose massive bulk had known the workmanship and perhaps the worship of living and thinking creatures.

Dazed and frightened, yet not without a certain thrill of the scientist's or archaeologist's delight, I examined my surroundings more closely.

The moon, now near the zenith, shone weirdly and vividly above the towering steeps that hemmed in the chasm, and revealed the fact that a far-flung body of water flowed at the bottom, winding out of sight in both directions, and almost lapping my feet as I stood on the slope.

Across the chasm, the wavelets washed the base of the Cyclopean monolith; on whose surface I could now trace both inscriptions and crude sculptures. The writing was in a system of hieroglyphics unknown to me, and unlike anything I had ever seen in books; consisting for the most part of conventionalized aquatic symbols such as fishes, eels, octopi, crustaceans, molluscs, whales, and the like.

It was the pictorial carving, however, that did most to hold me spellbound. Plainly visible across the intervening water on account of their enormous size, were an array of bas-reliefs whose subjects would have excited the envy of a Doré. I think that these things were supposed to depict men—at least, a certain sort of men; though the creatures were shown disporting like fishes in the waters of some marine grotto, or paying homage at some monolithic shrine which appeared to be under the waves as well. Of their faces and forms I dare not speak in detail; for the mere remembrance makes me grow faint. Grotesque beyond the imagination of a Poe or a Bulwer, they were damnably human in general outline despite webbed hands and feet, shockingly wide and flabby lips, glassy, bulging eyes, and other features less pleasant to recall. Curiously enough, they seemed to have been chiseled badly out of proportion with their scenic background; for one of the creatures was shown in the act of killing a whale represented as but little larger than himself.

I remarked, as I say, their grotesqueness and strange size; but in a moment decided that they were merely the imaginary gods of some primitive fishing or seafaring tribe; some tribe whose last descendant had perished eras before the first ancestor of the Piltdown or Neanderthal man was born. Awestruck at this unexpected glimpse into a past beyond the conception of the most daring anthropologist, I stood musing, whilst the moon cast queer reflections on the silent channel before me.

Then suddenly I saw it. With only a slight churning to mark its rise to the surface, the thing slid into view above the dark waters. Vast, Polyphemus-like, and loathsome, it darted like a stupendous monster of nightmares to the monolith, about which it flung its gigantic scaly arms, the while it bowed its hideous head and gave vent to certain measured sounds. I think I went mad then.

Of my frantic ascent of the slope and cliff, and of my delirious journey back to the stranded boat, I remember little. I believe I sang a great deal, and laughed oddly when I was unable to sing. I have indistinct recollections of a great storm some time after I reached the boat; at any rate, I know that I heard peals of thunder, and other tones which Nature utters only in wild and terrible moods.

★ ★ ★

WHEN I CAME OUT OF THE SHADOWS I was in a San Francisco hospital; brought thither by the captain of the American ship which had picked up my boat in mid-ocean. In my delirium I had said much, but found that my words had been given scant attention. Of any land upheaval in the Pacific, my rescuers knew nothing; nor did I deem it necessary to insist upon a thing which I knew they could not believe. Once I sought out a celebrated ethnologist, and amused him with peculiar questions regarding the ancient Philistine legend of Dagon, the Fish-God; but, soon perceiving that he was hopelessly conventional, I did not press my inquiries.

It is at night, especially when the moon is gibbous and waning, that I see the thing. I tried morphine, but the drug has given only transient surcease, and has drawn me into its clutches as a hopeless slave. So now I am going to end matters, having written a full account for the information or the contemptuous amusement of my fellow-men. Often I ask myself if it could not all have been a pure phantasm—a mere freak of fever as I lay sun-stricken and raving in the open boat after my escape from the German man-of-war.

This I ask myself, but ever does there come before me a hideously vivid vision in reply. I cannot think of the deep sea without shuddering at the nameless things that may at this very moment be crawling and floundering on its slimy bed, worshipping their ancient stone idols and carving their own detestable likenesses on submarine obelisks of water-soaked granite. I dream of a day when they may rise above the billows to drag down in their reeking talons the remnants of puny, war-exhausted mankind—of a day when the land shall sink, and the dark ocean floor shall ascend amidst universal pandemonium.

The end is near. I hear a noise at the door, as of some immense slippery body lumbering against it. It shall not find me. God, *that hand!* The window! The window!

THE END

GATHERING THE LAST WOOD

(for Rose and Ron)

Before the fall tourists wander loudly by
and muzzle season winnows the wood
comes time for winter kindling.

On the crossroad in a field of brown fern,
surrounded by the family maple grove,
stands an old working sugar shack.

And I've been scouring the countryside
and gathering sugar wood today,
the last pieces for the first fires.

When sap's running and the arch is heating.
this wood will burn fast and furious,
giving years and heart for me.

Nothing special about sweet wood, really.
Ten running cord cut inch fine and dried
will do the season short.

By now the woodshed's stacked dry and full
of maple, birch, and beech wood limbs
waiting to boil the sap down.

But this afternoon deep in the first frost nights
and warm days of September promise,
I find myself wonderfully apart.

Yet gladly do I look about and share the wood
with a squirrel taking flight
and a far off crow.

I walk a maple line as much to walk as gather,
cherishing the sounds of silence,
and seeing sugar fire.

—Patty Summers
12 September 2003

I PAINTED ONLY TERROR!

FASTER! FASTER!

PAUL BEAUMONT, BUILT HIS FAME WITH HIS PAINTINGS OF HUMAN TERROR! AND THEN HE PLANNED HIS MASTERPIECE! NOTHING WOULD STOP HIM-- NOT EVEN THOUGH IT COST THE LIFE OF HIS BEAUTIFUL MODEL! HOW COULD PAUL BEAUMONT KNOW THE GRISELY RETRIBUTION THAT WOULD COME...

AFTER THIS JOB, I'M GOING TO PAINT IT! THE PICTURE OF A PERSON MORE FRIGHTENED THAN ANYONE HAS BEEN BEFORE! HA! HA! HA! MY MASTERPIECE!

DOC, I CAN'T SLEEP! I'M HAVING MONSTROUS NIGHTMARES! AS YOU MAY KNOW I'M AN ARTIST WHO SPECIALIZES IN PORTRAITS OF TERROR!

I AM WELL ACQUAINTED WITH YOUR WORK. YOU'RE A HIGHLY RESPECTED ARTIST!

HOW DID YOU BECOME OBSESSED WITH THE TOPIC OF TERROR AS THE MAIN SUBJECT OF YOUR WORK?

I ALWAYS LIKED TO STUDY TERROR! IT... IT FASCINATED ME! I REMEMBER THE FIRST PAINTING I DID! I PAINTED A WOMAN'S FACE FROM MEMORY! I WAS IN A CROWD, WATCHING A FIRE, AND THERE WAS A WOMAN IN A BURNING WINDOW...

HELP! HELP!

MY PICTURE OF THAT WOMAN MADE A HIT! ...I DISCOVERED I'M GOOD AT PAINTING THAT SORT OF THING! I GOT A CHANCE TO SEE A MAN ELECTROCUTED! I'LL NEVER FORGET THE WAY HE LOOKED WHEN HE FIRST SAW THE CHAIR...

I'VE PAINTED HUNDREDS OF THAT KIND OF PICTURE! I'M FAMOUS! BUT, DOC... I'M GETTING TOO NERVOUS! DOC, WHAT'S WRONG WITH ME?

FEAR IS COMMUNICABLE! YOU'VE DABBLED IN IT TOO MUCH! I'D ADVISE YOU TO GIVE UP PAINTING THINGS LIKE THAT! TRY PAINTING PRETTY FARM SCENES... A RIVER! BIRDS IN THE TREES!
DOC, ARE YOU CRAZY?

ME, PAINT THINGS LIKE THAT? HA! HA! THAT'S FUNNY! WHY... I PAINT ONLY TERROR!
YOU HAD BETTER STOP BEFORE IT'S TOO LATE, MR. BEAUMONT!

OKAY, DOC, THAT'S WHAT I'LL DO! I'LL GO RIGHT HOME AND PAINT A PICTURE OF MAMA BIRD FEEDING LITTLE BABY BIRD! GOOD IDEA! THANKS FOR THE ADVICE! HA! HA!

BACK AT HOME, THAT EVENING...
THAT DOC THINKS I'M CRAZY! WHAT A LAUGH!

...BUT HE'S RIGHT, IT'S MAKING ME NERVOUS! I KNOW WHAT I'LL DO-- I'LL PAINT JUST ONE SUPREME MASTERPIECE! IT'LL BRING ME FAME ALL OVER THE WORLD!

...NOW WHAT I'LL NEED IS A BEAUTIFUL YOUNG GIRL MODEL! I'LL TELL HER NOTHING! THEN I'LL FRIGHTEN HER -- OH, I'LL FRIGHTEN HER, ALL RIGHT...

PAUL BEAUMONT LIVED IN A SUBURBAN COTTAGE, WITH HIS ELDERLY HOUSEKEEPER! BUT THE OLD WOMAN WAS AWAY THIS WEEK! HE MADE HIS DIABOLICAL PREPARATIONS!
...MY HIGH-SPEED CAMERA, HIDDEN! WHEN I GET HER REALLY FRIGHTENED, IT'LL SNAP A CLOSEUP OF HER FACE!...

I'LL HAVE THAT SNAPSHOT OF HOW SHE LOOKS, AS TERRIFIED AS ANYBODY CAN BE! THEN I'LL PAINT FROM THE PHOTOGRAPH! I'LL PUT THE AD IN TOMORROW!

AND, AS FATE WOULD HAVE IT...
I'M SURE SICK OF WORKIN' IN THE FIVE AN' TEN!
I'M GOOD LOOKIN', WHY COULDN'T I BE A MODEL!

BOX 432!
MODEL WANTED.
GOOD PAY. NO EX-
PERIENCE NEC-
ESSARY. APPLY
JOHN ALLEN,
RIVER ROAD.
THIS LOOKS LIKE ITS WORTH A TRY!

THAT SAME EVENING...
HMMM, SORTA LIKE-- A HAUNTED HOUSE! OH, WELL!

YOU SAW MY AD? COME IN, MY DEAR!
T-THANK YOU!

IT SEEMED SIMPLE ENOUGH-- POSING FOR AN ARTIST WHO WANTED TO PAINT HER PICTURE!
YES, I THINK THAT YOU WILL DO! WE'LL START NOW! YOU'LL FIND YOUR COSTUME IN THE DRESSING ROOM!
OH! ALL RIGHT, SIR!

AND PRESENTLY...
I'M READY, MR. BEAUMONT!

OH, GOOD! I'LL BE WITH YOU IN A MINUTE!

TO THE UNSUSPECTING GIRL IT WAS A GRISLY, TERRIBLE SHOCK! SHE STOOD TRANSFIXED, WITH THE BLOOD DRAINING FROM HER FACE AND HER HEART RACING!
AAAAIIEE!

GRRRR... NOW MY CAMERA WILL PHOTOGRAPH HER FACE! OH, SHE'S FRIGHTENED ALL NIGHT!

THEN, SUDDENLY, BEAUMONT FELT HER GO LIMP IN HIS GRIP! HE DID NOT REALIZE WHAT HAD HAPPENED! HE WAS LAUGHING WILDLY WITH EXCITEMENT AS HIS CAMERA CLICKED...
...GOT IT! JUST PERFECT...

AND IN ANOTHER MOMENT...
WH...WHY-- SHE'S DEAD! I FRIGHTENED HER TO DEATH!

THE ULTIMATE OF HUMAN TERROR! TRIUMPH SURGED IN BEAUMONT! HE BURIED THE BODY OUT IN THE DARK, LONELY WOODS NEAR HIS COTTAGE...
NOW I'LL DEVELOP THE PHOTOGRAPH AND PAINT MY MASTERPIECE FROM IT!

IN THE LITTLE DARK ROOM IN HIS CELLAR...
IT'S COMING OUT PERFECTLY. THAT GIRL SAID SHE WAS NEW IN TOWN-- NO FAMILY-- NO FRIENDS-- NO ONE WILL EVEN MISS HER!

AT MIDNIGHT HE WAS READY! BUT, SUDDENLY...
WHA--?! NO! NO-- IT CAN'T BE! YOU'RE DEAD AND BURIED! I'M JUST IMAGINING THINGS!
DEAD-- YES! BUT YOU'VE GOT YOUR MASTERPIECE TO PAINT! REMEMBER?

PAINT IT! PAINT IT! YOU WANT A PICTURE OF HUMAN TERROR? GO ON, PAINT IT!
YES, OF COURSE I WILL! MY MASTERPIECE! HA! NOBODY WILL EVER PAINT A PICTURE OF TERROR LIKE THIS ONE!

THE HOURS PASSED...THROUGH THE NIGHT... AND WHEN THE DAWN CAME...
DON'T STOP, I TELL YOU! KEEP GOING! YOUR MASTERPIECE, REMEMBER?
YES! YES! HA! IT'S PERFECT! PERFECT!

THE STUDIO DOOR WAS LOCKED. AFTER A MOMENT, THE OLD WOMAN RAN FOR THE POLICE! AND...
IT'S ALL FINISHED! HA! HA! HO! HO! HO!
WE BETTER BREAK DOWN THE DOOR, CLANCY!
YEAH!

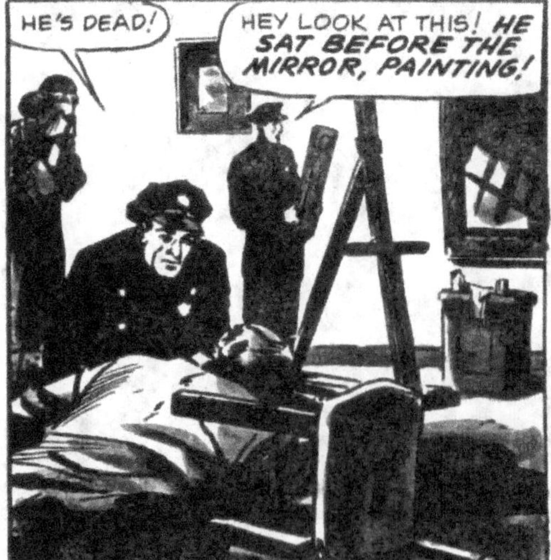
HE'S DEAD!
HEY LOOK AT THIS! HE SAT BEFORE THE MIRROR, PAINTING!

EARLY THAT MORNING, BEAUMONT'S OLD HOUSEKEEPER UNEXPECTEDLY RETURNED...
IT'S ALMOST DONE NOW! SURE, I'M FRIGHTENED! OH, I'M FRIGHTENED ALL RIGHT! THAT MAKES IT EVEN BETTER, DOESN'T IT? HA! HA! HA!
...HE'S GONE OUT OF HIS MIND!...

THEN THERE WAS A CRASH INSIDE THE STUDIO, AND, AS THE POLICEMEN BROKE IN...
MR. BEAUMONT! MR. BEAUMONT!... NO!

HIS SUPREME MASTERPIECE...AS HE SAT BEFORE THE MIRROR! HIS... SELF PORTRAIT!
The End

THE BRIDGE OF SAN LUIS REY

BY THORNTON WILDER

PART THREE:
ESTEBAN

ONE MORNING TWIN BOYS WERE DIS-covered in the foundlings' basket before the door of the Convent of Santa María Rosa de las Rosas. Names were found for them almost before the arrival of the wet-nurse, but the names were not as useful to them as our names are to most of us, for no one ever succeeded in telling the boys apart. There was no way of knowing who their parents were, but Limean gossips, noticing as the boys grew older how straight they held themselves and how silent and sombre they were, declared them to be Castilian and laid them in turn at all sorts of crested doorways. The person in the world who came nearest to being their guardian was the Abbess of the Convent. Madre María del Pilar had come to hate all men, but she grew fond of Manuel and Esteban. In the late afternoon she would call them into her office, send for some cakes from the kitchen, and tell them stories about the Cid and Judas Maccabeus and the thirty-six misfortunes of Harlequin. She grew to love them so, that she would catch herself gazing deep into their black and frowning eyes, looking for those traits that would appear when they grew to be men, all that ugliness, all that soullessness that made hideous the world she worked in. They grew up about the convent until they were a little past the age when their presence began to be a slight distraction to the dedicated sisters. From thence they became vaguely attached to all the sacristies in town: they trimmed all the cloister hedges; they polished every possible crucifix; they passed a damp cloth once a year over most of the ecclesiastical ceilings. All Lima knew them well. When the priest rushed through the streets carrying his precious burden into a sickroom either Esteban or Manuel was to be seen striding behind him, swinging a censer. As they grew older, however, they showed no desire for the clerical life. They gradually assumed the profession of the scribe. There were few printing presses in the New World and the boys soon made a fair living transcribing comedies for the theatre, ballads for the crowds, and advertisements for the merchants. Above all they were the copyists of the choirmasters and made endless parts of the motets of Morales and Vittoria.

Because they had no family, because they were twins, and because they were brought up by women, they were silent. There was in them a curious shame in regard to their resemblance. They had to live in a world where it was the subject of continual comment and joking. It was never funny to them and they suffered the eternal pleasantries with stolid patience. From the years when they first learned to speak they invented a secret language for themselves, one that was scarcely dependent on the Spanish for its vocabulary, or even for its syntax. They resorted to it only when they were alone, or at great intervals in moments of stress whispered it in the presence of others. The Archbishop of Lima was something of a philologist; he dabbled in dialects; he had even evolved quite a brilliant table for the vowel and consonant changes from Latin into Spanish and from Spanish into Indian-Spanish. He was storing up notebooks of quaint lore against an amusing old age he planned to offer himself back on his estates outside Segovia. So when he heard one day about the secret language of the twin brothers, he trimmed some quills and sent for them. The boys stood humiliated upon the rich carpets of his study while he tried to extract from them their *bread* and *tree* and their *I see* and *I saw*. They did not know why the experience was I so horrible to them. They bled. Long shocked silences followed each of the Archbishop's questions, until finally one or the other mumbled an answer. The priest thought for a while that they were merely in awe before his rank and before the luxury of his apartment, but at last, much perplexed, he divined the presence of some deeper reluctance and sadly let them go.

This language was the symbol of their profound identity with one another, for just as resignation was a word insufficient to describe the spiritual change that came over the Marquesa de Montemayor on that night in the inn at Cluxambuqua, so *love* is inadequate to describe the tacit almost ashamed oneness of these brothers. What relationship is it in which few words are exchanged, and those only about the details of food, clothing and occupation; in which the two persons have a curious reluctance even to glance at one another; and in which there is a tacit arrangement not to appear together in the city and to go on the same errand by different streets? And yet side by side with this there existed a need of one another so terrible that it produced miracles as naturally as the charged air of a sultry day produces lightning. The brothers were scarcely aware of it themselves, but telepathy was a common occurrence in their lives, and when one returned home the other was always aware of it when his brother was still several streets away.

Suddenly they discovered that they were tired of writing. They went down to the sea and found an occupation in loading and unloading vessels, not ashamed of working side by side with Indians. They drove teams across the provinces. They picked fruit. They were ferrymen. And always they were silent. Their sombre faces took on from these labors a male and gypsy cast. Their hair was seldom cut and under the dark mat their eyes looked up suddenly surprised and a little sullen. All the world was remote and strange and hostile except one's brother.

But at last the first shadow fell across this unity and the shadow was cast by the love of women. They had returned to the city and resumed the copying of parts for the theatre. One night the manager, foreseeing a thinning house, gave them a free admission. The boys did not like what they found there. Even speech was for them a debased form of silence; how much more futile is poetry which is a debased form of speech. All those allusions to honour, reputation, and the flame of love, all the metaphors about birds, Achilles and the jewels of Ceylon were fatiguing. In the presence of literature they had the same darkling intelligence that stirs for a time behind the eyes of a dog, but they sat on patiently, gazing at the bright candles and the rich clothes. Between the acts of the comedy the Perichole stepped out of her rôle, put on twelve petticoats and danced before the curtain. Esteban had some copying still to do, or pretended so, and went home early; but Manuel stayed on. The red stockings and shoes of the Perichole had made their impression.

Both brothers had fetched and carried their manuscripts up and down the dusty stairs behind the stage. There they had seen an irritable girl in a soiled bodice mending her stockings before a mirror while her stage director read aloud her lines for memorization. She had let fall upon the boys for a moment the detonation of her amazing eyes, immediately dissipated in her amused recognition that they were twins. Forthwith she had dragged them into the room and placed them side by side. Carefully, amusedly and remorselessly she had peered into every square inch of their faces, until finally laying one hand on Esteban's shoulder she had cried out: "This one is the younger!" That had been several years before and neither brother had thought of the episode again.

Henceforth all Manuel's errands seemed to lead him past the theatre. Late at night he would drift about among the trees beneath her dressing-room window. It was not the first time that Manuel had been fascinated by a woman (both brothers had possessed women, and often, especially during their years at the waterfront; but simply, latinly), but it was the first time that his will and imagination had been thus overwhelmed. He had lost that privilege of simple nature, the dissociation of love and pleasure. Pleasure was no longer as simple as eating; it was being complicated by love. Now was beginning that crazy loss of one's self, that neglect of everything but one's dramatic thoughts about the beloved, that feverish inner life all turning upon the Perichole and which would so have astonished and disgusted her had she been permitted to divine it. This Manuel had not fallen in love through any imitation of literature. It was not of him, at all events, that the bitterest tongue in France had remarked only fifty years before: that many people would never have fallen in love if they had not heard about it. Manuel read little; he had only been once to the theatre (where above all there reigns the legend that love is a devotion) and the Peruvian tavern-songs that he might have heard, unlike those of Spain, reflected very little of the romantic cult of an idealized woman. When he said over to himself that she was beautiful and rich and fatiguingly witty and the Viceroy's mistress, none of these attributes that made her less obtainable had the power to quench his curious and tender excitement. So he leaned against the trees in the dark, his knuckles between his teeth, and listened to his loud heart-beats.

But the life that Esteban was leading had been full enough for him. There was no room in his imagination for a new loyalty, not because his heart was less large than Manuel's, but because it was of a simpler texture. Now he discovered that secret from which one never quite recovers, that even in the most perfect love one person loves less profoundly than the other. There may be two equally good, equally gifted, equally beautiful, but there may never be two that love one another equally well. So Esteban sat up in their room by a guttering candle, his knuckles between his teeth, and wondered why Manuel was so changed and why the whole meaning had gone out of their life.

One evening Manuel was stopped on the street by a small boy who announced to him that the Perichole wished him to call upon her at once. Manuel turned in his path and went to the theatre. Straight, sombre and impersonal, he entered the actress's room and stood waiting. Camila had a service to ask of Manuel and she thought a few preliminary blandishments were necessary, but she scarcely paused in combing a blond wig that was dressed upon the table before her.

"You write letters for people, don't you? I want you to write a letter for me, please. Please come in."

He came forward two steps.

"You never pay me the least visit either of you. That's not Spanish of you."—meaning 'courteous.'—"Which are you, Manuel or Esteban?"

"Manuel."

"It doesn't matter. You are both unfriendly. Neither of you ever comes to see me. Here I sit learning stupid lines all day and no one ever comes to see me but a lot of peddlers. It is because I am an actress, no?"

This was not very artful, but for Manuel it was unspeakably complicated. He merely stared at her from the shadows of his long hair and left her to improvise.

"I am going to engage you to write a letter for me, a very secret letter. But now I can see that you don't like me and that to ask you to write a letter would be as good as reading it aloud in all the wine-shops. What does that look mean, Manuel? Are you my friend?"

"Yes, señora."

"Go away. Send me Esteban. You do not even say *Yes, señora* as a friend would say it."

Long pause. Presently she raised her head: "Are you still there, Unfriendly?"

"Yes, señora ... you can trust me to do anything for you ... you can trust ..."

"If I ask you to write one letter for me, or two letters, you promise never to mention to a human being what is in them, or even that you wrote them?"

"Yes, señora."

"What do you promise by?—by the Virgin Mary?"

"Yes, señora."

"And by the heart of Saint Rose of Lima?"

"Yes, señora."

"Name of the Name, Manuel, anyone would think you were as

stupid as an ox. Manuel, I am very angry with you. You are not stupid. You don't look stupid. Please don't say just *Yes, señora* again. Don't be stupid or I'll send for Esteban. Is anything the matter with you?"

Here Manuel cast himself upon the Spanish language and exclaimed with unnecessary vigor: "I swear by the Virgin Mary and the heart of St. Rose of Lima that all that has to do with the letter will be secret."

"Even from Esteban," prompted the Perichole.

"Even from Esteban."

"Well, that's better." She motioned him to sit down at a table where writing materials were already laid out. As she dictated she strode about the room, frowning, swinging her hips. With her arms akimbo, she hugged her shawl about her shoulders defiantly.

«*Camila Perichole kisses the hands of Your Excellency and says*—No, take another piece of paper and begin again. *The señora Micaela Villegas, artist, kisses the hands of Your Excellency and says that, being the victim of the envious and lying friends that Y. E.'s goodness permits about Him, she can no longer endure Y. E.'s suspicions and jealousy. Y. E.'s servant has always valued Y. E.'s friendship and has never committed, nor even thought, an offense against it, but she can no longer fight against the calumnies that Y. E. believes so readily. Señora Villegas, artist, called the Perichole, therefore returns herewith such of Y. E.'s gifts as have not been placed beyond recall, since without Y. E.'s confidence, Y. E.'s servant can take no pleasure in them.*"

Camila continued walking about the room for several minutes, consumed by her thoughts. Presently without so much as glancing at her secretary, she commanded: "Take another leaf. *Have you gone mad? Do not ever think of eating another bull to me again. It has caused a frightful war. Heaven protect you, my colt. Friday night, the same place, the same time. I may be a little late, for the fox is wide-awake.* That will be all."

Manuel rose.

"You swear that you have made no errors?"

"Yes, I swear."

"There is your money."

Manuel took the money.

"I shall want you to write me more letters from time to time. My uncle Pio generally writes my letters; these I do not wish him to know about. Good night. Go with God."

"Go with God."

Manuel descended the stairs and stood for a long time among the trees, not thinking, not moving.

Esteban knew that his brother was continually brooding over the Perichole, but he never suspected that he saw her. From time to time during the next two months a small boy would approach him in great haste and ask whether he were Manuel or Esteban, and being informed that he was only Esteban, the boy would add that Manuel was wanted at the theatre. Esteban assumed that the call was for copyist's work and was therefore utterly unprepared for a visit that they received one night in their room.

It was almost midnight. Esteban had gone to bed, and lay gazing out from under the blanket at the candle beside which his brother was working. There was a light tap at the door and Manuel opened to admit a lady heavily veiled, out of breath and nervous. She threw back the scarf from her face and said hurriedly:

"Quick, ink and paper. You are Manuel, yes? You must do a letter for me at once."

For a moment her glance fell on the two bright eyes that glared at her from the edge of the cot. She murmured: "Eu ... you must excuse me. I know it is late. It was necessary ... I must come." Then turning to Manuel, she whispered into his ear: "Write this: *I Perichole, am not accustomed to wait at a rendez-vous.* Have you finished that? *You are only a cholo, and there are better matadors than you, even in Lima. I am half Castilian and there are no better actresses in the world. You shall not have the opportunity*—Have you got that?—*to keep me waiting again, cholo, and I shall laugh the last, for even an actress does not grow old as fast as a bullfighter.*"

To Esteban in the shadows the picture of Camila leaning over his brother's hand and whispering into his ear was complete evidence that a new congeniality had formed such as he would never know. He seemed to shrink away into space, infinitely tiny, infinitely unwanted. He took one more glance at the tableau of love, all the paradise from which he was shut out, and turned his face to the wall.

Camila seized the note the moment it was done, pushed a coin along the table and in a last flurry of black lace, scarlet beads and excited whispers left the room. Manuel turned from the door with his candle. He sat down, put his hand over his ears, his elbows on his knees. He worshipped her. He murmured to himself over and over again that he worshipped her, making of the sound a sort of incantation and an obstacle to thought.

He emptied his mind of everything but a singsong, and it was this vacancy that permitted him to become aware of Esteban's mood. He seemed to hear a voice that proceeded from the shadows saying: "Go and follow her, Manuel. Don't stay here. You'll be happy. There's room for us all in the world." Then the realization became even more intense and he received a mental image of Esteban going a long way off and saying good-bye many times as he went. He was filled with terror; by the light of it he saw that all the other attachments in the world were shadows, or the illusions of fever, even Madre María del Pilar, even the Perichole. He could not understand why Esteban's misery should present itself as demanding a choice between him and the Perichole, but he could understand Esteban's misery, as misery. And at once he sacrificed everything to it, if it can be said we ever sacrifice anything save what we know we can never attain, or what some secret wisdom tells us it would be uncomfortable or saddening to possess. To be sure there was nothing on which Esteban could base a complaint. It was not jealousy, for in their earlier affairs it had never occurred to either of them that their loyalty to one another had been diminished. It was merely that in the heart of one of them there was left room for an elaborate imaginative attachment and in the heart of the other there was not. Manuel could not quite understand this and, as we shall see, he nourished a dim sense of being accused unjustly. But he did understand that Esteban was suffering. In his excitement he groped for a means of holding this brother who seemed to be receding into the distance. And at once, in one unhesitating stroke of the will, he removed the Perichole from his heart.

He blew out the candle and lay down on his bed. He was trembling. He said aloud with exaggerated casualness: "Well, that's the last letter I write for that woman. She can go and find a pander somewhere else. If ever she calls here or sends for me when I'm out, tell her so. Make it plain. That's the last I have to do with her," and with that he began reciting his evening psalm aloud. But he had hardly reached *A sagitta volante in die* when he became aware that Esteban had risen and was lighting the candle.

"What's the matter?" he asked.

"I'm going out for a walk," replied Esteban sombrely, fastening his belt. After a moment, he broke out with an assumption of anger: "You don't have to say ... what you just said, for me. I don't care whether you write her letters or not. You don't have to change for me. I haven't anything to do with that."

"Go to bed, you fool. God, you're a fool, Esteban. What made you think I said that, for you? Don't you believe I mean it when I say I'm through with her? Do you think I want to write any

more of her dirty letters and get paid for them like that?"

"It's all right. You love her. You don't have to change because of me."

"'*Love* her?' *Love* her? You're crazy, Esteban. How could I love her? What chance would there be for me? Do you suppose she'd give me those letters to write if there were any chance? Do you suppose she'd push a piece of money across the table every time.... You're crazy, Esteban, that's all."

There was a long pause. Esteban would not go to bed. He sat by the candle in the middle of the room, tapping with his hand on the edge of the table.

"Go to bed, you fool," shouted Manuel, rising on one elbow under the blanket. He was talking in their secret language and the new pain at his heart, gave a greater ring of reality to his assumption of rage. "I'm all right."

"I won't. I'm going out for a walk," replied Esteban picking up his coat.

"You can't go out for a walk. It's two o'clock. It's raining. You can't go and walk about for hours like that. Look, Esteban, I swear to you there's nothing left to all that. I don't love her. I only did for a time."

By now Esteban stood in the dark of the open door. In the unnatural voice with which we make the greatest declarations of our lives, he muttered: "I'm in your way," and turned to go.

Manuel leapt out of his bed. His head seemed to be full of a great din, a voice crying out that Esteban was going away forever, was leaving him alone forever. "In the name of God, in the name of God, Esteban, come back here."

Esteban came back and went to bed and the matter was not mentioned again for many weeks. The very next evening Manuel had an opportunity of declaring his position. A messenger arrived from the Perichole and was told harshly to inform the actress that Manuel would write no more letters for her.

ONE EVENING MANUEL TORE OPEN the flesh on his knee against a piece of metal.

Neither brother had ever been ill for as much as a day in his life, and now Manuel, utterly bewildered, watched his leg swell and felt the waves of pain rise and fall in his body. Esteban sat by and stared at his face trying to imagine what great pain was. At last one midnight Manuel remembered that the signboard of a certain hairdresser in the city described the proprietor as an experienced barber and surgeon. Esteban ran through the streets to fetch him. He pounded on the door. Presently a woman leaned out of a window and announced that her husband would be back in the morning. During the fearful hours that followed, they told one another that when the doctor had seen the leg all would be well. He would do something about it, and Manuel would be out around the town in a day or two, even in a day perhaps, even less than a day.

The barber arrived and prescribed various draughts and ointments. Esteban was instructed to lay cold cloths on his brother's leg every hour. The barber withdrew and the brothers sat down to wait for the pain to subside. But while they continued staring into one another's face waiting for the miracle of science the pain grew worse. Hour after hour Esteban approached with his dripping towel and they discovered that the moment of its application was the worst of all. With all the fortitude in the world Manuel could not prevent himself from shouting and from flinging himself about upon the bed. Night came on and still Esteban stolidly waited and watched and worked. Nine, ten, eleven. Now when the time drew near to apply the cloths (the hour struck so musically from all those towers) Manuel would plead with Esteban not to do his work. He would resort to guile and declare that he scarcely felt it. But Esteban, his heart bursting with pain and his lips a line of iron, would roll back the blanket and bind the towel fiercely in its place. Manuel gradually became delirious and under this application all the thoughts he did not permit himself in his right mind would burst magnified from his mouth.

Finally at two o'clock, out of his mind with rage and pain, and flinging himself half out of the bed until his head struck the floor, Manuel cried: "God condemn your soul to the hottest hell there is. A thousand devils torture you forever, Esteban. God condemn your soul, do you hear?" At first, the air gone out of his body, Esteban went out into the hall and leaned against the door, his mouth and eyes wide open. Still he heard from within: "Yes, Esteban, may God damn your beastly soul forever, do you hear that? For coming between me and what was mine by right. She was mine, do you hear, and what right had you...." and he would go off into an elaborate description of the Perichole.

These outbursts recurred hourly. It was some time before Esteban was able to realize that his brother's mind was not then clear. After some moments of horror, in which his being a devout believer had its part, he would return to the room and go about his duties with bent head.

Towards dawn his brother became serener. (For what human ill does not dawn seem to be an alleviation?) It was in one of these intervals that Manuel said quite calmly:

"God's son! I feel better, Esteban. Those cloths must be good after all. You'll see. I'll be up and around tomorrow. You haven't slept for days. You'll see I won't cause you any more trouble, Esteban."

"It's no trouble, you fool."

"You mustn't take me seriously when I try and stop you putting on the old cloths, Esteban."

A long pause. At last Esteban brought out, barely audible:

"I think ... don't you think it would be fine if I sent for the Perichole? She could just come and see you for a few minutes, I mean...."

"Her? You still thinking about her? I wouldn't have her here for anything. No."

But Esteban was not content yet. He dragged up a few more phrases from the very centre of his being:

"Manuel, you still feel, don't you, that I came between you and the Perichole and you don't remember that I told you it was all right with me. I swear to you I'd have been glad if you'd gone away with her, or anything."

"What are you bringing that up for, Esteban? I tell you, in God's own name, I never think of that. She's nothing to me. When are you going to forget that, Esteban? I tell you I'm glad things are as they are. Look, I got to get angry when you keep going back to that."

"Manuel, I wouldn't speak of it again, only when you get angry at me about the cloths ... you, you get angry at me about that, too. And you talk about it and you ..."

"Look, I'm not responsible what I say. My old leg hurts then, see."

"Then you don't damn me to hell because ... it looks like I came between you and the Perichole?"

"Damn you to ...? What makes you say that? You're going crazy, Esteban; you're imagining things. You haven't had any sleep, Esteban. I been a curse to you and you're losing your health because of me. But you'll see, I won't trouble you much more. How could I damn you to hell, Esteban, when you're all I've got? Understand, see, that when the cold cloths go on, I just lose myself, see. You know. Don't think about it twice. It's time to put them on now. I won't say a word."

"No, Manuel, I'll skip this time. It won't do you any harm, I'll just skip this time."

"I've got to get well, Esteban. I've got to get up soon, you know. Put them on. But one minute—give me the crucifix. I swear by the blood and body of Christ that if I say anything against Esteban, I don't mean it and it's just the foolish words when I'm dreaming because of the pain in my leg. God make me well again soon, amen. Put it back. There. Now I'm ready."

"Look, Manuel, it won't hurt if I skip just this once, see. It'll be good for you, sure, to not get it all stirred up just this once."

"No, I've got to get well. The doctor said it had to be done. I won't say a word, Esteban."

And it would begin all over again. During the second night a prostitute in the next room started beating on the wall, outraged at such language. A priest in the room on the other side would come out into the hall and beat on the door. The whole floor would gather before the room in exasperation. The innkeeper came up the stairs, loudly promising his guests that the brothers would be dumped into the street the very next morning. Esteban, holding his candle, would go into the hall and permit them to rage at him for as long as they pleased; but after that he took to pressing his hand firmly over his brother's mouth during the moments of greatest stress. This increased Manuel's personal rage at him and he would babble all through the night.

On the third night, Esteban sent for the priest and amidst the enormous shadows Manuel received the sacrament, and died.

Thereafter Esteban refused to come near the building. He would start off upon long walks, but presently drifting back, would hang about, staring at passers-by, within two streets of where his brother lay. The innkeeper failing to make any impression upon him and remembering that the boys were brought up at the Convent of Santa María Rosa de las Rosas, sent for the Abbess. Simply and soundly she directed all that was to be done. At last she went down to the street corner and spoke to Esteban. He watched her approach him, a glance mixed of longing and distrust. But when she stood near him he turned sideways and looked away.

"I want you to help me. Won't you come in and see your brother? Won't you come in and help me?"

"No."

"You won't help me!" A long pause. Suddenly as she stood there full of her helplessness there flashed through her mind an incident of many years before: the twin brothers about fifteen years old were sitting at her knee and she was telling them the story of the crucifixion. Their large grave eyes were fixed upon her lips. Suddenly Manuel had cried out loudly: "If Esteban and I had been there we would have prevented it."

"Well, then, if you won't help me, will you tell me which you are?"

"Manuel," said Esteban.

"Manuel, won't you come and sit with me up there for just a short time?"

After a long pause: "No."

"But Manuel, dear Manuel, can't you remember as children how you did so many things for me? You were willing to go across the town on some little errand. When I was ill you made the cook let you bring me my soup?" Another woman would have said: "Do you remember how much I did for you?"

"Yes."

"I, too, Manuel have lost. I too … once. We know that God has taken them into His hands…." But this did not do at all. Esteban turned vaguely and walked away from her. When he had gone about twenty paces he stopped and stared down a side-street, like a dog who wants to go away, but is reluctant to offend the master who calls him back.

That was all they could get out of him. When the fearful procession passed through the city, with its black hoods and masks, its candles in broad daylight, its display of heaped-up skulls, its terrifying psalms, Esteban followed it in the parallel streets, catching glimpses of it from a distance, like a savage.

All Lima was interested in this separation of the brothers. Housewives whispered together sympathetically about it as they unfurled their carpets from the balconies. The men in the wineshops, alluding to it, shook their heads and smoked in silence for a while. Travellers from the interior told of seeing Esteban as he strayed with eyes like coals along the dried-up beds of rivers or through the great ruins of the old race. A herder of llamas had come upon him standing upon a hilltop, asleep or dazed, wet with dew under the stars. Some fishermen surprised him swimming far out from shore. From time to time he would find work to do, he would become a shepherd or a carter, but after a few months he would disappear and stride from province to province. But he always returned to Lima. One day he appeared at the door of the Perichole's dressing-room; he made as though to speak, gazed earnestly at her and vanished. One day a sister came running into the office of Madre María del Pilar with the news that Esteban (whom the world called Manuel) was lingering about the door of the convent. The Abbess hurried out into the street. For months she had been asking herself what strategy could reconcile this half-demented boy to living among them again. She assembled as grave and calm a manner as she was able and appearing at the street door murmured "My friend" and looked at him. He gazed back at her with the same glance of longing and distrust that he had shown her before, and stood trembling. Again she whispered "My friend" and moved a step forward. Suddenly Esteban turned and breaking into a run disappeared. Madre María del Pilar rushed stumbling back to her desk and fell upon her knees, exclaiming angrily: "I have prayed for wisdom and You have given me none. You have not chosen to give me the least grace. I am a mere scrubber of floors…." But during the penance she set herself for this impudence the thought came to her to send for Captain Alvarado. Three weeks later she had a ten-minute conversation with him. And the next day he started for Cuzco where, it was said,

Esteban was doing some copying for the University.

There was this strange and noble figure in Peru during these years, the Captain Alvarado, the traveller. He was blackened and cured by all weathers. He stood in the Square with feet apart as though they were planted on a shifting deck. His eyes were strange, unaccustomed to the shorter range, too used to seizing the appearances of a constellation between a cloud and a cloud, and the outline of a cape in rain. His reticence was sufficiently explained for most of us by his voyages, but the Marquesa de Montemayor had other light on the matter. *"Captain Alvarado is bringing you this letter in person,"* she wrote to her daughter. *"Introduce him to some of your geographers, my treasure, though it may make them a little uncomfortable, for he is the diamond of sincerity. They will never see anyone who has travelled so far. Last night he described to me some of his voyages. Imagine him pushing his prow through a sea of weeds, stirring up a cloud of fish like grasshoppers in June; or sailing between islands of ice. Oh, he has been to China and up the rivers of Africa. But he is not merely an adventurer and he seems to take no pride in discovering new places; nor is he a mere merchant. One day I asked him narrowly why he lived so, and he avoided my question. I found out from my laundress what I think is the reason of his wandering: My child, he had a child; my daughter, he had a daughter. She was just old enough to cook a holiday meal, and do a little sewing for him. In those days he merely sailed between Mexico and Peru and hundreds of times she waved him farewell or welcome. We have no way of knowing whether she was more beautiful or intelligent than the thousands of other girls that lived about him, but she was his. I suppose it seems ignoble to you that a great oak of a man should go about the world like a blind man about an empty house merely because a chit of a girl has been withdrawn from it. No, no, you cannot understand this, my adored one, but I understand and grow pale. Last night he sat with me and talked of her. He laid his cheek against his hand and looking into the fire, he said: 'It sometimes seems to me that she is away upon a voyage and that I shall see her again. It seems to me that she is in England.' You will laugh at me, but I think he goes about the hemispheres to pass the time between now and his old age."*

The brothers had always entertained a great respect for Captain Alvarado. They had worked for him a short time and the silence of the three of them had made a little kernel of sense in a world of boasting, self-excuse and rhetoric. So now when the great traveller came into the dark kitchen where Esteban was eating the boy drew his chair farther into the shadow, but at a distance, he was glad. The Captain gave no sign of recognizing or even of seeing him until he had finished his meal. Esteban had finished long before, but not wishing to be spoken to, waited until the Captain should have left the cave. At last the Captain walked over to him and said:

"You are Esteban or Manuel. You helped me once with some unloading. I am Captain Alvarado."

"Yes," said Esteban.

"How are you?"

Esteban muttered something.

"I am looking for some strong fellows to go on my next trip with me." Pause. "Would you like to come?" Longer pause. "England. And Russia.... Hard work. Good wages.... A long way from Peru.—Well?"

Apparently Esteban had not been listening. He sat with his eyes on the table. At last the Captain raised his voice, as to a deaf person:

"I said: Do you want to go on my next trip with me...."

"Yes, I'll go," answered Esteban suddenly.

"Fine. That's fine. I want your brother, too, of course."

"No."

"What's the matter? Wouldn't he want to come?"

Esteban mumbled something, looking away. Then half rising, he said: "I got to go now. I've got to see somebody about something."

"Let me see your brother myself. Where is he?"

"... 'dead," said Esteban.

"Oh, I didn't know. I didn't know. I'm sorry." "Yes," said Esteban. "I got to go."

"Hmm.—Which are you? What's your name?"

"Esteban."

"When did Manuel die?"

"Oh, just a ... just a few weeks. He hit his knee against something and ... just a few weeks ago."

They both kept their eyes on the floor.

"How old are you, Esteban?"

"Twenty-two."

"Well, that's settled then, you're coming with me?"

"Yes."

"You may not be used to the cold."

"Yes, I'm used to it.—I've got to go now. I got to go in the city and see somebody about something."

"Well, Esteban. Come back here for supper and we'll talk about the trip. Come back and have some wine with me, see. Will you?"

"Yes, I will."

"Go with God."

"Go with God."

They had supper together and it was arranged that they were to start for Lima the next morning. The Captain got him very drunk. At first they poured and drank and poured and drank in silence. Then the Captain began to talk about ships and their courses. He asked Esteban questions about tackle and about the guide-stars. Then Esteban began to talk about other things, and to talk very loudly:

"On the ship you must give me something to do all the time. I'll do anything, anything. I'll climb up high and fix ropes; and I'll watch all night,—because, you know, I don't sleep well anyway. And, Captain Alvarado, on the ship you must pretend that you don't know me. Pretend that you hate me the most. So that you'll always give me things to do. I can't sit still and write at a table any more.—And don't tell the other men about me ... that is, about ..."

"I hear you went into a burning house, Esteban, and pulled someone out."

"Yes. I didn't get burned or anything. You know," cried Esteban, leaning across the table, "you're not allowed to kill yourself; you know you're not allowed. Everybody knows that. But if you jump into a burning house to save somebody, that wouldn't be killing yourself. And if you became a matador and the bull caught you that wouldn't be killing yourself. Only you mustn't put yourself in the bull's way on purpose. Did you ever notice that animals never kill themselves, even when they're sure to lose? They never jump into a river or anything, even when they're sure to lose. Some people say that horses run into bonfires. Is that true?"

"No, I don't think that's true."

"I don't think it's true. We had a dog once. Well, I mustn't think of that.—Captain Alvarado, do you know Madre María del Pilar?"

"Yes."

"I want to give her a present before I go away. Captain Alvarado, I want you to give me all my wages before I start—I won't need any money anywhere—and I want to buy her a present now. The present isn't from me only. She was ... was ..." Here Esteban wished to say his brother's name, but was unable to. Instead he continued in a lower voice: "She had a kind of a ... she had a serious loss, once. She said so. I don't know who it was, and I want to give her a present. Women can't bear that kind of a thing like we can."

The Captain promised him that they would choose something in the morning. Esteban talked about it at great length. At last the Captain saw him slip under the table, and himself, rising up, went out into the square before the inn. He looked at the line of the Andes and at the streams of stars crowding forever across the sky. And there was that wraith hanging in mid-air and smiling at him, the wraith with the silvery voice that said for the thousandth time: "Don't be gone long. But I'll be a big girl when you get back." Then he went within and carried Esteban to his room and sat looking at him for a long while.

The next morning he was waiting at the bottom of the stairs when Esteban appeared:

"We're starting when you're ready," said the Captain.

The strange glitter had returned to the boy's eyes. He blurted out: "No, I'm not coming. I'm not coming after all."

«Aïe! Esteban! But you have promised me that you would come."

"It's impossible. I can't come with you," and he turned back up the stairs.

"Come here a moment, Esteban, just a moment."

"I can't come with you. I can't leave Peru."

"I want to tell you something."

Esteban came down to the foot of the stairs.

"How about that present for Madre María del Pilar?" asked the Captain in a low voice. Esteban was silent, looking over the mountains. "You aren't going to take that present away from her? It might mean a lot to her ... you know."

"All right," murmured Esteban, as though much impressed.

"Yes. Besides the ocean's better than Peru. You know Lima and Cuzco and the road. You have nothing more to know about them. You see it's the ocean you want. Besides on the boat you'll have something to do every minute. I'll see to that. Go and get your things and we'll start."

Esteban was trying to make a decision. It had always been Manuel who had made the decisions and even Manuel had never been forced to make as great a one as this. Esteban went slowly upstairs. The Captain waited for him and waited so long that presently he ventured half the way up the stairs and listened. At first there was silence; then a series of noises that his imagination was able to identify at once. Esteban had scraped away the plaster about a beam and was adjusting a rope about it. The Captain stood on the stairs trembling: "Perhaps it's best," he said to himself. "Perhaps I should leave him alone. Perhaps it's the only thing possible for him." Then on hearing another sound he flung himself against the door, fell into the room and caught the boy. "Go away,"

cried Esteban. "Let me be. Don't come in now."

Esteban fell face downward upon the floor. "I am alone, alone, alone" he cried. The Captain stood above him, his great plain face ridged gray with pain; it was his own old hours he was reliving. He was the awkwardest speaker in the world apart from the lore of the sea, but there are times when it requires a high courage to speak the banal. He could not be sure the figure on the floor was listening, but he said "We do what we can. We push on, Esteban, as best we can. It isn't for long, you know. Time keeps going by. You'll be surprised at the way time passes."

They started for Lima. When they reached the bridge of San Luis Rey, the Captain descended to the stream below in order to supervise the passage of some merchandise, but Esteban crossed by the bridge and fell with it.

TO BE CONTINUED IN
LITERARY OUTLAW #3

GRAVES
GHOST HUNTER
BY B. CHRYSLER

LATE ONE WINTERS NIGHT, A PERSISTANT BELL RINGING BRINGS GRAVES TO THE DOOR . . .

A THREAT SIGNED WITH A CAT'S PAW.. I WOULDN'T WORRY ABOUT IT. SOME FRIEND PLAYING A JOKE.. GO HOME AND GET SOME SLEEP.

WHAT EVER YOU SHAY, GRAVES. THANKS!

NICE LI'L KITTY. YOU DIDN'T SEND ME THAT NASTY THREAT.. DID YOU...

SUDDENLY THE AIR CHILLS.. AND . . .

HUH! WHERE'D YOU COME FROM ?!

DON'T.. STOP! HELP! HELP!
THE NEXT MORNING...
HE'S DEAD ALL RIGHT! FIENDISHLY CLAWED WITH SOMETHING POISONOUS. SEE HOW THE MARKS TURNED BLUE, MR. GRAVES?
I'LL NEVER FORGIVE MYSELF! HE ASKED FOR HELP, BUT I THOUGHT IT WAS A HOAX!
THE NAME IN HIS WALLET SHOWS HE'S CHARLES WRIGHT, THE BANKER! WE'D BETTER PAY A VISIT TO HIS HOME!
I AM CLAUDE WRIGHT, CHARLES' BROTHER.. THIS IS MY FIANCEE, MISS GRANT.
HOWDY.
IT IS NOT THE FIRST VIOLENT DEATH IN OUR FAMILY, MR. GRAVES.. WAIT 'TIL YOU READ THE FAMILY HISTORY. WHILE IN INDIA MY FATHER WAS KILLED IN THE SAME MANNER! IT IS BELIEVED THAT HE HAD BEEN CLAWED TO DEATH BY SOME JUNGLE BEAST!
REALLY.
ONLY CATS AND WOMEN SCRATCH..
I HAVE A FEELING I'M TO BE THE NEXT VICTIM!
CATS! AND THAT CAT IN THE YARD.. IT WALKS IN THE FRESH SNOW YET LEAVES NO TRACKS!

IT'S RUNNING AWAY! NOW WHAT WOULD A STRAY CAT BE DOING AROUND HERE?
WHAT'S THIS? LOOKS LIKE A NOTE!
I JUST GOT A REPORT FROM THE MEDICAL EXAMINER, MR. GRAVES. THAT POISON IN HIS BODY HASN'T BEEN IN USE FOR CENTURIES. THERE'S SOME LEGEND ABOUT WITCHES BREWING IT WAY BACK IN THE MIDDLE AGES!
THAT'S INTERESTING! I'M GOING INSIDE, BUT I SUGGEST YOU SEARCH THE GROUNDS THOROUGHLY...
no one in your family can escape punishment. The curse shall be fulfilled!
I'LL TELL HIM ABOUT THE NOTE AFTER I TAKE A LOOK AT THE FAMILY HISTORY. I'VE A HUNCH I MIGHT FIND SOMETHING IMPORTANT HERE..
THIS CURSE ON OUR FAMILY BEGAN IN 1745 WHEN HAROLD WRIGHT, A JUDGE IN NORTH SALEM, MASSACHUSETTS, PASSED SENTENCE ON AGNES HARRINGTON TO BE BURNED AT THE STAKE FOR PRACTICING WITCHCRAFT. SHE PROCLAIMED A CURSE ON HIS FAMILY UNTO THE LAST GENERATION...

SUDDENLY A MYSTERIOUS LIGHT FILLS THE ROOM.. AND...
INQUISITIVE, AREN'T YOU?! LET ME SHOW YOU SOMETHING ELSE!
YOU.. AGNES HARRINGTON!
WAIT.. I'LL FOLLOW YOU. WHAT IS IT YOU WANT TO SHOW ME?!
..TO THE SUN PORCH? WHAT COULD BE THERE?
GREAT SCOTT! MISS GRANT.. DEAD!
A FEW MINUTES LATER...
BUT HOW.. HOW? WE WERE ALL IN THE HOUSE...
I'M NEXT.. I KNOW IT! HELP ME! HELP ME!
HOW CAN I HELP HIM?
CLAUDE IS THE LAST OF THE FAMILY. WHEN HE DIES, MY CURSE IS FULFILLED.. BUT I MUST REMOVE GRAVES AS I DID THE GIRL!

I'M GOING TO TOWN. CONTINUE TO SEARCH THE GROUNDS FOR A TRACE OF THAT CAT. ACTUALLY IT'S A WITCH THAT WAS BURNED TO DEATH AT THE STAKE IN 1745!
HUH?!
LATER, GRAVES RETURNS.. TO THE WRIGHT LIBRARY...
I SHOULD HAVE A SPECIAL VISITOR SOON.
AH! THERE SHE IS.. SOONER THAN I EXPECTED! NOW TO TAKE MY DISINTEGRATOR AND FINISH HER OFF.. WHERE DID I PUT IT.. IT'S GONE!
GRAVES, YOU SHOULD HAVE KNOWN IF WE CROSSED PATHS, IT SPELLED DOOM FOR ONE OF US.. THAT ONE IS YOU!
COME NOW, I WAS PREPARED FOR MORE OF A STRUGGLE...
OW..W.. THOSE POISONED CLAWS...
IN A FEW SECONDS THE POISON WILL HAVE ITS EFFECT.. YOU'LL NOT ANNOY ME ANY MORE!

AND YOU, CLAUDE WRIGHT.. ARE NEXT.. AND LAST!
HELP! HELP!
THERE ISN'T ANY-ONE TO HELP YOU.. SNIVELING FOOL!
PLEASE.. MERCY.. SPARE ME!
BACK TO THE LAND OF SHADOWS WHERE YOU BELONG, WITCH!
IT'S LUCKY I FOUND MY DISINTEGRATOR. THAT WILL FINISH HER! I'M NOT DEAD AS SHE HOPED!
TAKE THAT RAY OFF ME, YOU DEVIL!
IN A SWIRL OF MIST, THE SPECTRE FADES.. AND GRAVES RUSHES TO THE AID OF HER WOULD BE VICTIM . . .
HOW CAN I EVER THANK YOU, MR. GRAVES?
BOSH! HOLD STEADY, NOW!
WHAT'S GOING ON HERE, MEN?
WHEN I RETURNED TO TOWN, IT WAS FOR AN ANTIDOTE TO THAT POISON. THAT'S WHAT I JUST GAVE CLAUDE. SHE WAS OUT TO GET ME, TOO, SO I SET A TRAP FOR HER.. IT WAS A TIGHT SPOT THOUGH, UNTIL I FOUND MY DISINTEGRATOR! SHE'LL NEVER RETURN.. I GUARANTEE THAT!
THANK HEAVENS! HE'S BROKEN THE FAMILY CURSE!
WELL, I'LL BE!
GRAVES THE GHOST HUNTER, SOLVES ANOTHER WEIRD CRIME OF THE SUPERNATURAL IN THE NEXT ISSUE OF CROWN Comics!

THE HANGING STRANGER

BY PHILIP K. DICK

ED HAD ALWAYS BEEN A PRACTICAL man, when he saw something was wrong he tried to correct it. Then one day he saw *it* hanging in the town square.

Five o'clock Ed Loyce washed up, tossed on his hat and coat, got his car out and headed across town toward his TV sales store. He was tired. His back and shoulders ached from digging dirt out of the basement and wheeling it into the back yard. But for a forty-year-old man he had done okay. Janet could get a new vase with the money he had saved; and he liked the idea of repairing the foundations himself!

It was getting dark. The setting sun cast long rays over the scurrying commuters, tired and grim-faced, women loaded down with bundles and packages, students swarming home from the university, mixing with clerks and businessmen and drab secretaries. He stopped his Packard for a red light and then started it up again. The store had been open without him; he'd arrive just in time to spell the help for dinner, go over the records of the day, maybe even close a couple of sales himself. He drove slowly past the small square of green in the center of the street, the town park. There were no parking places in front of LOYCE TV SALES AND SERVICE. He cursed under his breath and swung the car in a U-turn. Again he passed the little square of green with its lonely drinking fountain and bench and single lamppost.

From the lamppost something was hanging. A shapeless dark bundle, swinging a little with the wind. Like a dummy of some sort. Loyce rolled down his window and peered out. What the hell was it? A display of some kind? Sometimes the Chamber of Commerce put up displays in the square.

Again he made a U-turn and brought his car around. He passed the park and concentrated on the dark bundle. It wasn't a dummy. And if it was a display it was a strange kind. The hackles on his neck rose and he swallowed uneasily. Sweat slid out on his face and hands.

It was a body. A human body.

★ ★ ★

"LOOK AT IT!" LOYCE SNAPPED. "COME on out here!"

Don Fergusson came slowly out of the store, buttoning his pin-stripe coat with dignity. "This is a big deal, Ed. I can't just leave the guy standing there."

"See it?" Ed pointed into the gathering gloom. The lamppost jutted

up against the sky—the post and the bundle swinging from it. "There it is. How the hell long has it been there?" His voice rose excitedly. "What's wrong with everybody? They just walk on past!"

Don Fergusson lit a cigarette slowly. "Take it easy, old man. There must be a good reason, or it wouldn't be there."

"A reason! What kind of a reason?"

Fergusson shrugged. "Like the time the Traffic Safety Council put that wrecked Buick there. Some sort of civic thing. How would I know?"

Jack Potter from the shoe shop joined them. "What's up, boys?"

"There's a body hanging from the lamppost," Loyce said. "I'm going to call the cops."

"They must know about it," Potter said. "Or otherwise it wouldn't be there."

"I got to get back in." Fergusson headed back into the store. "Business before pleasure."

Loyce began to get hysterical. "You see it? You see it hanging there? A man's body! A dead man!"

"Sure, Ed. I saw it this afternoon when I went out for coffee."

"You mean it's been there all afternoon?"

"Sure. What's the matter?" Potter glanced at his watch. "Have to run. See you later, Ed."

Potter hurried off, joining the flow of people moving along the sidewalk. Men and women, passing by the park. A few glanced up curiously at the dark bundle—and then went on. Nobody stopped. Nobody paid any attention.

"I'm going nuts," Loyce whispered. He made his way to the curb and crossed out into traffic, among the cars. Horns honked angrily at him. He gained the curb and stepped up onto the little square of green.

The man had been middle-aged. His clothing was ripped and torn, a gray suit, splashed and caked with dried mud. A stranger. Loyce had never seen him before. Not a local man. His face was partly turned, away, and in the evening wind he spun a little, turning gently, silently. His skin was gouged and cut. Red gashes, deep scratches of congealed blood. A pair of steel-rimmed glasses hung from one ear, dangling foolishly. His eyes bulged. His mouth was open, tongue thick and ugly blue.

"For Heaven's sake," Loyce muttered, sickened. He pushed down his nausea and made his way back to the sidewalk. He was shaking all over, with revulsion—and fear.

Why? Who was the man? Why was he hanging there? What did it mean?

And—why didn't anybody notice?

He bumped into a small man hurrying along the sidewalk. "Watch it!" the man grated, "Oh, it's you, Ed."

Ed nodded dazedly. "Hello, Jenkins."

"What's the matter?" The stationery clerk caught Ed's arm. "You look sick."

"The body. There in the park."

"Sure, Ed." Jenkins led him into the alcove of LOYCE TV SALES AND SERVICE. "Take it easy."

Margaret Henderson from the jewelry store joined them. "Something wrong?"

"Ed's not feeling well."

Loyce yanked himself free. "How can you stand here? Don't you see it? For God's sake—"

"What's he talking about?" Margaret asked nervously.

"The body!" Ed shouted. "The body hanging there!"

More people collected. "Is he sick? It's Ed Loyce. You okay, Ed?"

"The body!" Loyce screamed, struggling to get past them. Hands caught at him. He tore loose. "Let me go! The police! Get the police!"

"Ed—"

"Better get a doctor!"

"He must be sick."

"Or drunk."

Loyce fought his way through the people. He stumbled and half fell. Through a blur he saw rows of faces, curious, concerned, anxious. Men and women halting to see what the disturbance was. He fought past them toward his store. He could see Fergusson inside talking to a man, showing him an Emerson TV set. Pete Foley in the back at the service counter, setting up a new Philco. Loyce shouted at them frantically. His voice was lost in the roar of traffic and the murmur around him.

"Do something!" he screamed. "Don't stand there! Do something! Something's wrong! Something's happened! Things are going on!"

The crowd melted respectfully for the two heavy-set cops moving efficiently toward Loyce.

"Name?" the cop with the notebook murmured.

"Loyce." He mopped his forehead wearily. "Edward C. Loyce. Listen to me. Back there—"

"Address?" the cop demanded. The police car moved swiftly through traffic, shooting among the cars and buses. Loyce sagged against the seat, exhausted and confused. He took a deep shuddering breath.

"1368 Hurst Road."

"That's here in Pikeville?"

"That's right." Loyce pulled himself up with a violent effort. "Listen to me. Back there. In the square. Hanging from the lamppost—"

"Where were you today?" the cop behind the wheel demanded.

"Where?" Loyce echoed.

"You weren't in your shop, were you?"

"No." He shook his head. "No, I was home. Down in the basement."

"In the *basement*?"

"Digging. A new foundation. Getting out the dirt to pour a cement frame. Why? What has that to do with—"

"Was anybody else down there with you?"

"No. My wife was downtown. My kids were at school." Loyce looked from one heavy-set cop to the other. Hope flicked across his face, wild hope. "You mean because I was down there I missed—the explanation? I didn't get in on it? Like everybody else?"

After a pause the cop with the notebook said: "That's right. You missed the explanation."

"Then it's official? The body—it's *supposed* to be hanging there?"

"It's supposed to be hanging there. For everybody to see."

Ed Loyce grinned weakly. "Good Lord. I guess I sort of went off the deep end. I thought maybe something had happened. You know, something like the Ku Klux Klan. Some kind of violence. Communists or Fascists taking over." He wiped his face with his breast-pocket handkerchief, his hands shaking. "I'm glad to know it's on the level."

"It's on the level." The police car was getting near the Hall of Justice. The sun had set. The streets were gloomy and dark. The lights had not yet come on.

"I feel better," Loyce said. "I was pretty excited there, for a minute. I guess I got all stirred up. Now that I understand, there's no need to take me in, is there?"

The two cops said nothing.

"I should be back at my store. The boys haven't had dinner. I'm all right, now. No more trouble. Is there any need of—"

"This won't take long," the cop behind the wheel interrupted. "A short process. Only a few minutes."

"I hope it's short," Loyce muttered. The car slowed down for a stoplight. "I guess I sort of disturbed the peace. Funny, getting excited like that and—"

Loyce yanked the door open. He sprawled out into the street and rolled to his feet. Cars were moving all around him, gaining speed as the light changed. Loyce leaped onto the curb and raced among the people, burrowing into the swarming crowds. Behind him he heard sounds, shouts, people running.

They weren't cops. He had realized that right away. He knew every cop in Pikeville. A man couldn't own a store, operate a business in a small town for twenty-five years without getting to know all the cops.

They weren't cops—and there hadn't been any explanation. Potter, Fergusson, Jenkins, none of them knew why it was there. They didn't know—and they didn't care. *That* was the strange part.

Loyce ducked into a hardware store. He raced toward the back, past the startled clerks and customers, into the shipping room and through the back door. He tripped over a garbage can and ran up a flight of concrete steps. He climbed over a fence and jumped down on the other side, gasping and panting.

There was no sound behind him. He had got away.

He was at the entrance of an alley, dark and strewn with boards and ruined boxes and tires. He could see the street at the far end. A street light wavered and came on. Men and women. Stores. Neon signs. Cars.

And to his right—the police station.

He was close, terribly close. Past the loading platform of a grocery store rose the white concrete side of the Hall of Justice. Barred windows. The police antenna. A great concrete wall rising up in the darkness. A bad place for him to be near. He was too close. He had to keep moving, get farther away from them.

Them?

Loyce moved cautiously down the alley. Beyond the police station was the City Hall, the old-fashioned yellow structure of wood and gilded brass and broad cement steps. He could see the endless rows of offices, dark windows, the cedars and beds of flowers on each side of the entrance.

And—something else.

Above the City Hall was a patch of darkness, a cone of gloom denser than the surrounding night. A prism of black that spread out and was lost into the sky.

He listened. Good God, he could hear something. Something that made him struggle frantically to close his ears, his mind, to shut out the sound.

A buzzing. A distant, muted hum like a great swarm of bees.

Loyce gazed up, rigid with horror. The splotch of darkness, hanging over the City Hall. Darkness so thick it seemed almost solid. *In the vortex something moved.* Flickering shapes. Things, descending from the sky, pausing momentarily above the City Hall, fluttering over it in a dense swarm and then dropping silently onto the roof.

Shapes. Fluttering shapes from the sky. From the crack of darkness that hung above him.

He was seeing—them.

FOR A LONG TIME LOYCE WATCHED, crouched behind a sagging fence in a pool of scummy water.

They were landing. Coming down in groups, landing on the roof of the City Hall and disappearing inside. They had wings. Like giant insects of some kind. They flew and fluttered and came to rest—and then crawled crab-fashion, sideways, across the roof and into the building.

He was sickened. And fascinated. Cold night wind blew around him and he shuddered. He was tired, dazed with shock. On the front steps of the City Hall were men, standing here and there. Groups of men coming out of the building and halting for a moment before going on.

Were there more of them?

It didn't seem possible. What he saw descending from the black chasm weren't men. They were alien—from some other world, some other dimension. Sliding through this slit, this break in the shell of the universe. Entering through this gap, winged insects from another realm of being.

On the steps of the City Hall a group of men broke up. A few moved toward a waiting car. One of the remaining shapes started to re-enter the City Hall. It changed its mind and turned to follow the others.

Loyce closed his eyes in horror. His senses reeled. He hung on tight, clutching at the sagging fence. The shape, the man-shape, had abruptly fluttered up and flapped after the others. It flew to the sidewalk and came to rest among them.

Pseudo-men. Imitation men. Insects with ability to disguise themselves as men. Like other insects familiar to Earth. Protective coloration. Mimicry.

Loyce pulled himself away. He got slowly to his feet. It was night. The alley was totally dark. But maybe they could see in the dark. Maybe darkness made no difference to them.

He left the alley cautiously and moved out onto the street. Men and women flowed past, but not so many, now. At the bus-stops stood waiting groups. A huge bus lumbered along the street, its lights flashing in the evening gloom.

Loyce moved forward. He pushed his way among those waiting and when the bus halted he boarded it and took a seat in the rear, by the door. A moment later the bus moved into life and rumbled down the street.

★ ★ ★

LOYCE RELAXED A LITTLE. HE STUDIED the people around him. Dulled, tired faces. People going home from work. Quite ordinary faces. None of them paid any attention to him. All sat quietly, sunk down in their seats, jiggling with the motion of the bus.

The man sitting next to him unfolded a newspaper. He began to read the sports section, his lips moving. An ordinary man. Blue suit. Tie. A businessman, or a salesman. On his way home to his wife and family.

Across the aisle a young woman, perhaps twenty. Dark eyes and hair, a package on her lap. Nylons and heels. Red coat and white angora sweater. Gazing absently ahead of her.

A high school boy in jeans and black jacket.

A great triple-chinned woman with an immense shopping bag loaded with packages and parcels. Her thick face dim with weariness.

Ordinary people. The kind that rode the bus every evening. Going home to their families. To dinner.

Going home—with their minds dead. Controlled, filmed over with the mask of an alien being that had appeared and taken possession of them, their town, their lives. Himself, too. Except that he happened to be deep in his cellar instead of in the store. Somehow, he had been overlooked. They had missed him. Their control wasn't perfect, foolproof.

Maybe there were others.

Hope flickered in Loyce. They weren't omnipotent. They had made a mistake, not got control of him. Their net, their field of control, had passed over him. He had emerged from his cellar as he had gone down. Apparently their power-zone was limited.

A few seats down the aisle a man was watching him. Loyce broke off his chain of thought. A slender man, with dark hair and a small mustache. Well-dressed, brown suit and shiny shoes. A book between his small hands. He was watching Loyce, studying him intently. He turned quickly away.

Loyce tensed. One of *them*? Or—another they had missed?

The man was watching him again. Small dark eyes, alive and clever. Shrewd. A man too shrewd for them—or one of the things itself, an alien insect from beyond.

The bus halted. An elderly man got on slowly and dropped his token into the box. He moved down the aisle and took a seat opposite Loyce.

The elderly man caught the sharp-eyed man's gaze. For a split second something passed between them.

A look rich with meaning.

Loyce got to his feet. The bus was moving. He ran to the door. One step down into the well. He yanked the emergency door release. The rubber door swung open.

"Hey!" the driver shouted, jamming on the brakes. "What the hell—"

Loyce squirmed through. The bus was slowing down. Houses on all sides. A residential district, lawns and tall apartment buildings. Behind him, the bright-eyed man had leaped up. The elderly man was also on his feet. They were coming after him.

Loyce leaped. He hit the pavement with terrific force and rolled against the curb. Pain lapped over him. Pain and a vast tide of blackness. Desperately, he fought it off. He struggled to his knees and then slid down again. The bus had stopped. People were getting off.

Loyce groped around. His fingers closed over something. A rock, lying in the gutter. He crawled to his feet, grunting with pain. A shape loomed before him. A man, the bright-eyed man with the book.

Loyce kicked. The man gasped and fell. Loyce brought the rock down. The man screamed and tried to roll away. "*Stop!* For God's sake listen—"

He struck again. A hideous crunching sound. The man's voice cut off and dissolved in a bubbling wail. Loyce scrambled up and back. The others were there, now. All around him. He ran, awkwardly, down the sidewalk, up a driveway. None of them followed him. They had stopped and were bending over the inert body of the man with the book, the bright-eyed man who had come after him.

Had he made a mistake?

But it was too late to worry about that. He had to get out—away from them. Out of Pikeville, beyond the crack of darkness, the rent between their world and his.

★ ★ ★

"Ed!" Janet Loyce backed away nervously. "What is it? What—"

Ed Loyce slammed the door behind him and came into the living room. "Pull down the shades. Quick."

Janet moved toward the window. "But—"

"Do as I say. Who else is here besides you?"

"Nobody. Just the twins. They're upstairs in their room. What's happened? You look so strange. Why are you home?"

Ed locked the front door. He prowled around the house, into the kitchen. From the drawer under the sink he slid out the big butcher knife and ran his finger along it. Sharp. Plenty sharp. He returned to the living room.

"Listen to me," he said. "I don't have much time. They know I escaped and they'll be looking for me."

"Escaped?" Janet's face twisted with bewilderment and fear. "Who?"

"The town has been taken over. They're in control. I've got it pretty well figured out. They started at the top, at the City Hall and police department. What they did with the *real* humans they—"

"What are you talking about?"

"We've been invaded. From some other universe, some other dimension. They're insects. Mimicry. And more. Power to control minds. Your mind."

"My mind?"

"Their entrance is *here*, in Pikeville. They've taken over all of you. The whole town—except me. We're up against an incredibly powerful enemy, but they have their limitations. That's our hope. They're limited! They can make mistakes!"

Janet shook her head. "I don't understand, Ed. You must be insane."

"Insane? No. Just lucky. If I hadn't been down in the basement I'd be like all the rest of you." Loyce peered out the window. "But I can't stand here talking. Get your coat."

"My coat?"

"We're getting out of here. Out of Pikeville. We've got to get help. Fight this thing. They *can* be beaten. They're not infallible. It's going to be close—but we may make it if we hurry. Come on!" He grabbed her arm roughly. "Get your coat and call the twins. We're all leaving. Don't stop to pack. There's no time for that."

White-faced, his wife moved toward the closet and got down her coat. "Where are we going?"

Ed pulled open the desk drawer and spilled the contents out onto the floor. He grabbed up a road map and spread it open. "They'll have the highway covered, of course. But there's a back road. To Oak Grove. I got onto it once. It's practically abandoned. Maybe they'll forget about it."

"The old Ranch Road? Good Lord—it's completely closed. Nobody's supposed to drive over it."

"I know." Ed thrust the map grimly into his coat. "That's our best chance. Now call down the twins and let's get going. Your car is full of gas, isn't it?"

Janet was dazed.

"The Chevy? I had it filled up yesterday afternoon." Janet moved toward the stairs. "Ed, I—"

"Call the twins!" Ed unlocked the front door and peered out. Nothing stirred. No sign of life. All right so far.

"Come on downstairs," Janet called in a wavering voice. "We're—going out for awhile."

"Now?" Tommy's voice came.

"Hurry up," Ed barked. "Get down here, both of you."

Tommy appeared at the top of the stairs. "I was doing my home work. We're starting fractions. Miss Parker says if we don't get this done—"

"You can forget about fractions." Ed grabbed his son as he came down the stairs and propelled him toward the door. "Where's Jim?"

"He's coming."

Jim started slowly down the stairs. "What's up, Dad?"

"We're going for a ride."

"A ride? Where?"

Ed turned to Janet. "We'll leave the lights on. And the TV set. Go turn it on." He pushed her toward the set. "So they'll think we're still—"

He heard the buzz. And dropped instantly, the long butcher knife out. Sickened, he saw it coming down the stairs at him, wings a blur of motion as it aimed itself. It still bore a vague resemblance to Jimmy. It was small, a baby one. A brief glimpse—the thing hurtling at him, cold, multi-lensed inhuman eyes. Wings, body still clothed in yellow T-shirt and jeans, the mimic outline still stamped on it. A strange half-turn of its body as it reached him. What was it doing?

A stinger.

Loyce stabbed wildly at it. It retreated, buzzing frantically. Loyce rolled and crawled toward the door. Tommy and Janet stood still as statues, faces blank. Watching without expression. Loyce stabbed again. This time the knife connected. The thing shrieked and faltered. It bounced against the wall and fluttered down.

Something lapped through his mind. A wall of force, energy, an alien mind probing into him. He was suddenly paralyzed. The mind entered his own, touched against him briefly, shockingly. An utterly alien presence, settling over him—and then it flickered out as the thing collapsed in a broken heap on the rug.

It was dead. He turned it over with his foot. It was an insect, a fly of some kind. Yellow T-shirt, jeans. His son Jimmy.... He closed his mind tight. It was too late to think about that. Savagely he scooped up his knife and headed toward the door. Janet and Tommy stood stone-still, neither of them moving.

The car was out. He'd never get through. They'd be waiting for him. It was ten miles on foot. Ten long miles over rough ground, gulleys and open fields and hills of uncut forest. He'd have to go alone.

Loyce opened the door. For a brief second he looked back at his wife and son. Then he slammed the door behind him and raced down the porch steps.

A moment later he was on his way, hurrying swiftly through the darkness toward the edge of town.

THE EARLY MORNING SUNLIGHT WAS blinding. Loyce halted, gasping for breath, swaying back and forth. Sweat ran down in his eyes. His clothing was torn, shredded by the brush and thorns through which he had crawled. Ten miles—on his hands and knees.

Crawling, creeping through the night. His shoes were mud-caked. He was scratched and limping, utterly exhausted.

But ahead of him lay Oak Grove.

He took a deep breath and started down the hill. Twice he stumbled and fell, picking himself up and trudging on. His ears rang. Everything receded and wavered. But he was there. He had got out, away from Pikeville.

A farmer in a field gaped at him. From a house a young woman watched in wonder. Loyce reached the road and turned onto it. Ahead of him was a gasoline station and a drive-in. A couple of trucks, some chickens pecking in the dirt, a dog tied with a string.

The white-clad attendant watched suspiciously as he dragged himself up to the station. "Thank God." He caught hold of the wall. "I didn't think I was going to make it. They followed me most of the way. I could hear them buzzing. Buzzing and flitting around behind me."

"What happened?" the attendant demanded. "You in a wreck? A hold-up?"

Loyce shook his head wearily. "They have the whole town. The City Hall and the police station. They hung a man from the lamppost. That was the first thing I saw. They've got all the roads blocked. I saw them hovering over the cars coming in. About four this morning I got beyond them. I knew it right away. I could feel them leave. And then the sun came up."

The attendant licked his lip nervously. "You're out of your head. I better get a doctor."

"Get me into Oak Grove," Loyce gasped. He sank down on the gravel. "We've got to get started—cleaning them out. Got to get started right away."

THEY KEPT A TAPE RECORDER GOING all the time he talked. When he had finished the Commissioner snapped off the recorder and got to his feet. He stood for a moment, deep in thought. Finally he got out his cigarettes and lit up slowly, a frown on his beefy face.

"You don't believe me," Loyce said.

The Commissioner offered him a cigarette. Loyce pushed it impatiently away. "Suit yourself." The Commissioner moved over to the window and stood for a time looking out at the town of Oak Grove. "I believe you," he said abruptly.

Loyce sagged. "Thank God."

"So you got away." The Commissioner shook his head. "You were down in your cellar instead of at work. A freak chance. One in a million."

Loyce sipped some of the black coffee they had brought him. "I have a theory," he murmured.

"What is it?"

"About them. Who they are. They take over one area at a time. Starting at the top—the highest level of authority. Working down from there in a widening circle. When they're firmly in control they go on to the next town. They spread, slowly, very gradually. I think it's been going on for a long time."

"A long time?"

"Thousands of years. I don't think it's new."

"Why do you say that?"

"When I was a kid.... A picture they showed us in Bible League. A religious picture—an old print. The enemy gods, defeated by Jehovah. Moloch, Beelzebub, Moab, Baalin, Ashtaroth—"

"So?"

"They were all represented by figures." Loyce looked up at the Commissioner. "Beelzebub was represented as—a giant fly."

The Commissioner grunted. "An old struggle."

"They've been defeated. The Bible is an account of their defeats. They make gains—but finally they're defeated."

"Why defeated?"

"They can't get everyone. They didn't get me. And they never got the Hebrews. The Hebrews carried the message to the whole world. The realization of the danger. The two men on the bus. I think they understood. Had escaped, like I did." He clenched his fists. "I killed one of them. I made a mistake. I was afraid to take a chance."

The Commissioner nodded. "Yes, they undoubtedly had escaped, as you did. Freak accidents. But the rest of the town was firmly in control." He turned from the window. "Well, Mr. Loyce. You seem to have figured everything out."

"Not everything. The hanging man. The dead man hanging from the lamppost. I don't understand that. *Why?* Why did they deliberately hang him there?"

"That would seem simple." The Commissioner smiled faintly. "*Bait.*"

Loyce stiffened. His heart stopped beating. "Bait? What do you mean?"

"To draw you out. Make you declare yourself. So they'd know who was under control—and who had escaped."

Loyce recoiled with horror. "Then they *expected* failures! They anticipated—" He broke off. "They were ready with a trap."

"And you showed yourself. You reacted. You made yourself known." The Commissioner abruptly moved toward the door. "Come along, Loyce. There's a lot to do. We must get moving. There's no time to waste."

Loyce started slowly to his feet, numbed. "And the man. *Who was the man?* I never saw him before. He wasn't a local man. He was a stranger. All muddy and dirty, his face cut, slashed—"

There was a strange look on the Commissioner's face as he answered. "Maybe," he said softly, "you'll understand that, too. Come along with me, Mr. Loyce." He held the door open, his eyes gleaming. Loyce caught a glimpse of the street in front of the police station. Policemen, a platform of some sort. A telephone pole—and a rope! "Right this way," the Commissioner said, smiling coldly.

★ ★ ★

As the sun set, the vice-president of the Oak Grove Merchants' Bank came up out of the vault, threw the heavy time locks, put on his hat and coat, and hurried outside onto the sidewalk. Only a few people were there, hurrying home to dinner.

"Good night," the guard said, locking the door after him.

"Good night," Clarence Mason murmured. He started along the street toward his car. He was tired. He had been working all day down in the vault, examining the lay-out of the safety deposit boxes to see if there was room for another tier. He was glad to be finished.

At the corner he halted. The street lights had not yet come on. The street was dim. Everything was vague. He looked around—and froze.

From the telephone pole in front of the police station, something large and shapeless hung. It moved a little with the wind.

What the hell was it?

Mason approached it warily. He wanted to get home. He was tired and hungry. He thought of his wife, his kids, a hot meal on the dinner table. But there was something about the dark bundle, something ominous and ugly. The light was bad; he couldn't tell what it was. Yet it drew him on, made him move closer for a better look. The shapeless thing made him uneasy. He was frightened by it. Frightened—and fascinated.

And the strange part was that nobody else seemed to notice it.

THE END

BLACK CAT

DUG FROM THE SANDS OF HISTORY, BY TIME'S INEXORABLE HAND, RENOWNED THROUGH THE AGES IS KHYBER PASS--- THE KEY TO INDIA'S BACK DOOR! DISPUTED FOR THOUSANDS OF YEARS PAST---AND AGAIN IN OUR TIME-- BLOODY, GREEDY CLAWS REACH OUT FROM THE FAR EAST TO---WELL, SUPPOSE YOU WATCH BLACK CAT FRUSTRATE THE "AMBUSH IN AFGHANISTAN"

SOUTH OF THE HINDU KISH--- WHERE FOOTHILLS OF THE HIMALAYAS COME DOWN TO EARTH,---IS THE LAND OF ROCKS AND STONES AND BLOODY FEUDS--

AFGHANISTAN
KHYBER PASS
KASHMIR
PESHAWAR
INDIA
BALUCHISTAN
INDUS RIVER
THAR DESERT
BOMBAY

MAJOR DOHAKI---IF OUR PINCER ON CHINA THROUGH INDIA IS TO SUCCEED ---THE KHYBER PASS MUST BE CLOSED AT ONCE! IS THIS UNDERSTOOD!

YISS, YOUR EXCELLENCY!

ONE WEEK LATER---

WOO-OOO-OOO.

GLAMOROUS LINDA TURNER AND HER FRIEND RICK HORNE, CORRESPONDENT...
IT SEEMS ONLY YESTERDAY THAT WE WERE IN BURMA--AND NOW WE'RE PERSIA BOUND!--PFF! JUST LIKE THAT!
I'VE GOT A ROOM IN CALIFORNIA JUST DYING FOR A REAL PERSIAN CARPET! LIFE CAN BE WONDERFUL, RICK!
A SPOT OF FOOD WOULD BE TOO, BEAUTIFUL LADY! I SAY, MAY I SHARE YOUR TABLE? WAR, Y'KNOW!
EEEEKKK! RICK! HE'S D-DEAD!
I SAY...YOU TWO ARE AMERICANS? HAVEN'T I SEEN YOU BEFORE, MISS? PLEASE DON'T THINK ME CHEEKY!
WHO HASN'T? ---MAY I PRESENT MISS LINDA TURNER! I'M RICK HORNE!
MY NAME IS-- AAAHHH-H-H
GOOD GRIEF! WHAT'S WRONG, MAN?
CRASH
OH, RICK-- THE POOR MAN--HE-
EASY, LINDA! WE CAN'T DO ANYTHING FOR THE POOR CHAP! LOOK HERE, I'D BETTER TAKE YOU TO YOUR COMPARTMENT!
MOMENTS LATER---
GO TO SLEEP, LINDA! WE ARRIVE AT PESHAWAR IN TWO HOURS! IT'S THE LAST STOP! I'M GOING BACK TO THE DINER--MAYBE A STORY IN ALL THIS! THAT BRITISHER LOOKED AS IF HE MIGHT BE IMPORTANT!
O.K., RICK, DON'T WORRY, I'LL SLEEP!
2

LIKE FISH I'LL SLEEP! HMM! THAT ENGLISHMAN WAS CARRYING A DIPLOMATIC POUCH! HE WAS POISONED, EH?---BY WHOM! AND---WHY?
I'LL SOON FIND OUT!
OR WILL I?
FURTIVELY--INSIDE---
YOU CAN'T DO THIS TO ME! I TELL YOU I'M RICK HORNE!
NO ONE'S BEING ALLOWED IN! GOOD! I CAN POKE ABOUT UNDISTURBED!
MOHAMMED HIMSELF COULD NOT ENTER! BAH! I DESPISE MY JOB ANYWAY! BAH!
MEANWHILE--
BROTHER, HUNGER GRIPS ME! LET ME PASS!
I'M RICK HORNE! I DEMAND YOU LET ME IN!
CAN YOU?
OOH-H!
YOU WISH TO SEE THE BRITISH DOG'S BODY? --AHA! THE WINDOW VER' CONVENIENT FOR THE SHE-VULTURE! ---NO! DO NOT MAKE MOVE!
SO YOU REMOVED THE EVIDENCE, EH! OH---YOU'RE NOT A MOHAMMEDAN! ---LEAST OF ALL A WOMAN! DROP THE DISGUISE, YOU JAP!
JAPANESE---AMERICAN DOG! WE DO NOT LIKE OUR RACIAL NAME VULGARIZED! ---UNDERSTAND?

NO, DON'T!
UG-OOOGH-H-H
I UNDERSTAND THIS!
I KILL YOU! YEOWWW!
YOU'VE GOT TO HAVE A PRIORITY, SAKI! I'M A PRETTY HEALTHY KID!
BUT YOU'RE NOT! TAKE IT, PUNK!
V-OOOPH!
OHH! I M-MUST STOP THIS!
CLANG
EMERGENCY CORD
CRAFTILY...AS BLACKCAT FOR THE MOMENT, IS SENT HELPLESSLY OFF BALANCE--
IMMEDIATELY AFTER---
GONE! VANISHED LIKE A GHOST--WELL,---BEFORE I'M THROUGH WITH HIM, HE'LL BE ONE! MEANWHILE I'D BETTER CHANGE BEFORE SOMEONE COMES!
WOT IN---'H'I SYE! SOME BLOKE'S YANKED THE EMERGENCY CORD!-WE'RE STOPPIN'!
SCREEEK-K-K
T-TRICKED
HA, HA!

MORNING...
PESHAWAR LAST STOP
COME ON, CUT THE ACT! FIFTEEN POUNDS TO TAKE US BOTH ACROSS AFGHANISTAN TO IRAN! AND NOT ONE RUPEE MORE!
IT IS GREAT ROBBERY THEE ASKS! --THY PURSE HAS SHARP TEETH!
HMM! HE'S NOT SO DUMB, RICK! LET ME TALK TO HIM!
DOG OF A DOG! THY HEART IS STONE, THY EYES PIGGISH, THY SOUL GARBAGE! ACCURSED IS THY LOT! THOU ART DOOMED IF THOU REFUSE US! I AM THE SHE-CHILD OF A WONDROUS AMERICAN CHIEF! HE WILL SEND WARRIORS! WILT TAKE US, DOG?
HEYAHH! TURN OFF THY SHRIEK, SHE-HYENA! FIFTEEN POUNDS IT SHALL BE!
ENGLISH SPOKEN GOOG
LINDA, YOU ARE WONDERFUL! YOU SCARED THE WITS OUT OF HIM!
I NEEDED SOME ACTING PRACTICE, RICK! WELL, IRAN-- HERE WE COME!
NOT FAR OFF, HOWEVER---
ME, DOHAKI, TO DRESS LIKE A WOMAN! PFUI!
WELL!? -- IS EVERYTHING PREPARED? EH, -- YOU LOW BORN DOGS?
YISS,-- MAJOR DOHAKI, ALL IS NOW PREPARED!
ALL ISS IN READINESS!
VERY WELL! YOUR DUTY IS TO HOLD THIS PASS BELOW! YOU WILL DIE AT YOUR POSTS IF NECESSARY! THE BRITISH MUST BE DENIED THE USE OF THIS PASS! UNDERSTAND!
MEANWHILE--- CLANKING THROUGH CHAOTICALLY HILLY COUNTRY---
CAP'N, SIR -- WOT IN BLOOMIN' THUNDER'RE WE DOIN' IN THIS KHYBER COUNTRY?

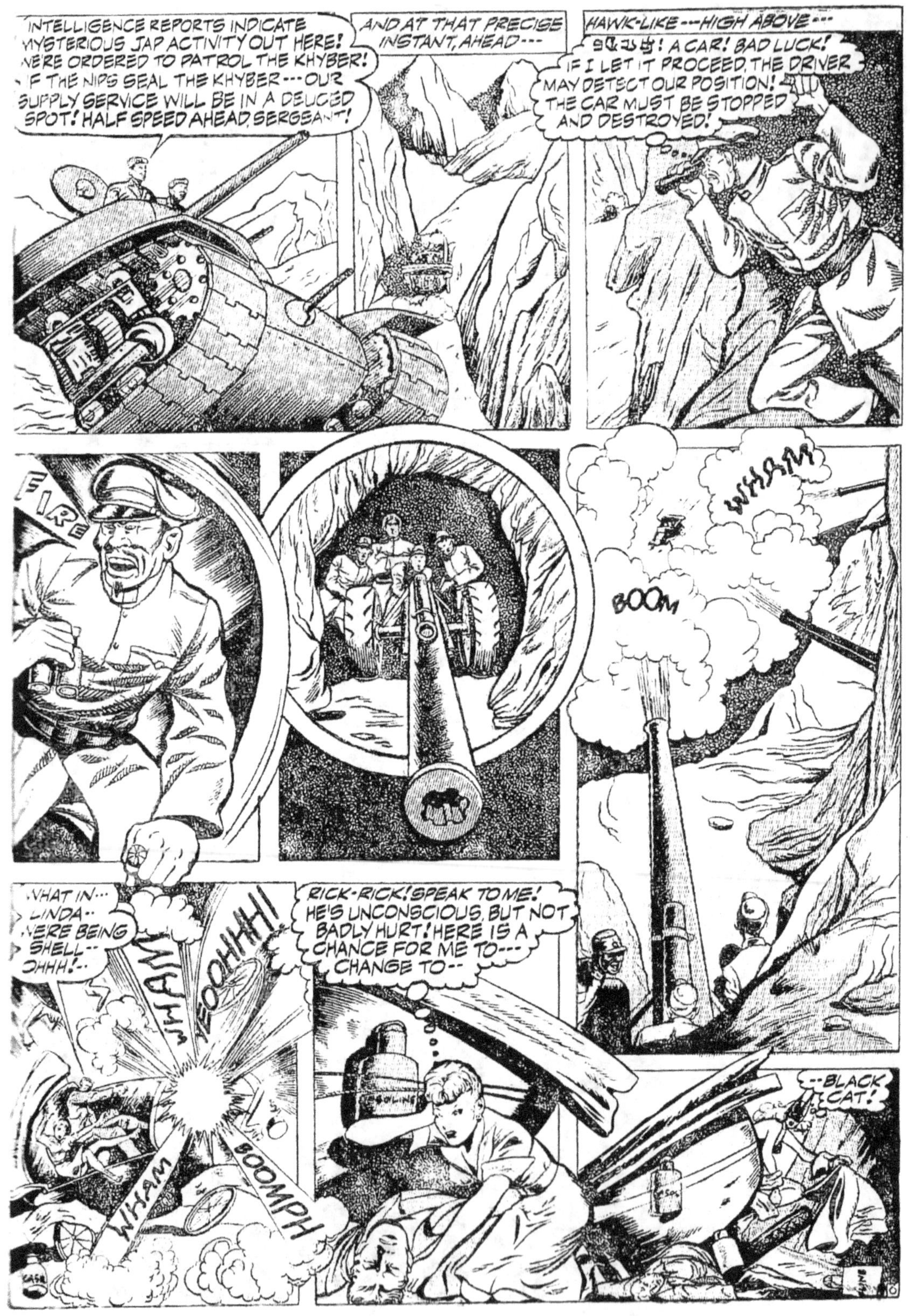
INTELLIGENCE REPORTS INDICATE MYSTERIOUS JAP ACTIVITY OUT HERE! WE'RE ORDERED TO PATROL THE KHYBER! IF THE NIPS SEAL THE KHYBER---OUR SUPPLY SERVICE WILL BE IN A DEUCED SPOT! HALF SPEED AHEAD, SERGEANT!
AND AT THAT PRECISE INSTANT, AHEAD---
HAWK-LIKE---HIGH ABOVE---
SO! A CAR! BAD LUCK! IF I LET IT PROCEED, THE DRIVER MAY DETECT OUR POSITION! THE CAR MUST BE STOPPED AND DESTROYED!
FIRE
WHRAM
BOOM
WHAT IN... LINDA... WE'RE BEING SHELL--- OHHH!--
WHAM
EEOOHHH!
BOOMPH
WHAM
RICK-RICK! SPEAK TO ME! HE'S UNCONSCIOUS, BUT NOT BADLY HURT! HERE IS A CHANCE FOR ME TO--- CHANGE TO--
GASOLINE
---BLACK CAT!

GREAT CATASTROPHE! --DO MY EYES DECEIVE ME, OR--- IT IS A JAP OFFICER UP THERE! SO THAT'S WHO--HMM! CLEVERLY CONCEALED HEAVY GUN BATTERIES, EH?---
THEN---
GUNFIRE! FROM THE DIRECTION OF TH' KHYBER! COLUMN, FULL SPEED AHEAD! PREPARE FOR ACTION!
DEVIL-MAY-CARE! -- CASUALLY CARELESS OF LIFE, --- LIBERTY'S LISSOME LASS!
THIS MAY WORK OUT AS I PLAN (Pant) OR, IT MAY WORK ME OUT AS IT PLANS! PFEW!
TANKS! BRITISH DOGS ARE COMING! ATTENTION-- GUNNERS! WATCH FOR MY SIGNAL! PREPARE TO FIRE!
WHILE UP ABOVE, A RECKLESS PLAN BEARS DANGEROUS FRUIT!---
NOW! FIRE! DESTROY THE BRITISH!
B-BRITISH! AND THE JAPS BELOW ME HAVE THEM IN A BIG BARN SIZE BULLS EYE!
A DIRECT HIT! SPREAD OUT! DISPERSE!
CRASH
BOOM
THOSE TANKS HAVEN'T A CHANCE AGAINST FIELD GUNS--UNLESS I REMEDY THAT LITTLE DETAIL!

I'LL SCOTCH THAT AMBUSH OF YOURS!--- RATS!
WHA- WHAT ISS?
AI-EE!
AIEE-EE! FLAMING GASOLINE CANS!
FLAMING DISASTER!
YAAA...!
AS DIZZILY HIGH ON THE CLIFF-LEDGE, DEADLY CONFLICT! AN AMAZED LONDONER--
WHAT THE DEUCE IS--? BLACK CAT! SHE'S HOOKED THE NIP COMMANDER!
(Pant, Pant) YOU D-DIE!
OH!
REALLY?
YAAA...!
NOW TO SKIP OUT OF HERE AND CHANGE BACK TO THE -BEAUTIFUL-BUT-DUMB- LINDA TURNER!
NOT MUCH LATER
WH-WHAT HAPPENED--? ...MY HEAD! (GASP)-- LINDA! ARE YOU OKAY?
I SAY---! HAVE YOU TWO SEEN BLACK C--? LINDA TURNER! WAIT 'TIL MY MEN SEE YOU! I SHALL HAVE A GREAT DISCIPLINARY PROBLEM!
NOT THE WAY YOU FELLOWS HAVE BEEN WINNING THE WAR!
HA! NO ONE NOTICED! MY LUCK'S STILL SHINY! BUT WILL IT ALWAYS BE?
FOLLOW THE ADVENTURES OF "BLACK CAT" IN THE NEXT ISSUE OF BLACK CAT COMICS!!

THE ADVENTURES OF PENROD

BY BOOTH TARKINGTON

CHAPTER 1
A BOY AND HIS DOG

PENROD SAT MOROSELY UPON THE back fence and gazed with envy at Duke, his wistful dog.

A bitter soul dominated the various curved and angular surfaces known by a careless world as the face of Penrod Schofield. Except in solitude, that face was almost always cryptic and emotionless; for Penrod had come into his twelfth year wearing an expression carefully trained to be inscrutable. Since the world was sure to misunderstand everything, mere defensive instinct prompted him to give it as little as possible to lay hold upon. Nothing is more impenetrable than the face of a boy who has learned this, and Penrod's was habitually as fathomless as the depth of his hatred this morning for the literary activities of Mrs. Lora Rewbush—an almost universally respected fellow citizen, a lady of charitable and poetic inclinations, and one of his own mother's most intimate friends.

Mrs. Lora Rewbush had written something which she called "The Children's Pageant of the Table Round," and it was to be performed in public that very afternoon at the Women's Arts and Guild Hall for the benefit of the Coloured Infants' Betterment Society. And if any flavour of sweetness remained in the nature of Penrod Schofield after the dismal trials of the school-week just past, that problematic, infinitesimal remnant was made pungent acid by the imminence of his destiny to form a prominent feature of the spectacle, and to declaim the loathsome sentiments of a character named upon the programme the Child Sir Lancelot.

After each rehearsal he had plotted escape, and only ten days earlier there had been a glimmer of light: Mrs. Lora Rewbush caught a very bad cold, and it was hoped it might develop into pneumonia; but she recovered so quickly that not even a rehearsal of the Children's Pageant was postponed. Darkness closed in. Penrod had rather vaguely debated plans for a self-mutilation such as would make his appearance as the Child Sir Lancelot inexpedient on public grounds; it was a heroic and attractive thought, but the results of some extremely sketchy preliminary experiments caused him to abandon it.

There was no escape; and at last his hour was hard upon him. Therefore he brooded on the fence and gazed with envy at his wistful Duke.

The dog's name was undescriptive of his person, which was obviously the result of a singular series of mesalliances. He wore a grizzled moustache and indefinite whiskers; he was small and shabby, and looked like an old postman. Penrod envied Duke because he was sure Duke would never be compelled to be a Child Sir Lancelot. He thought a dog free and unshackled to go or come as the wind listeth. Penrod forgot the life he led Duke.

There was a long soliloquy upon the fence, a plaintive monologue without words: the boy's thoughts were adjectives, but they were expressed by a running film of pictures in his mind's eye, morbidly prophetic of the hideosities before him. Finally he spoke aloud, with such spleen that Duke rose from his haunches and lifted one ear in keen anxiety.

> *"I hight Sir Lancelot du Lake, the Child,*
> *Gentul-hearted, meek, and mild.*
> *What though I'm but a littul child,*
> *Gentul-hearted, meek, and——' oof!"*

All of this except "oof" was a quotation from the Child Sir Lancelot, as conceived by Mrs. Lora Rewbush. Choking upon it, Penrod slid down from the fence, and with slow and thoughtful steps entered a one-storied wing of the stable, consisting of a single apartment, floored with cement and used as a storeroom for broken bric-a-brac, old paint-buckets, decayed garden-hose, worn-out carpets, dead furniture, and other condemned odds and ends not yet considered hopeless enough to be given away.

In one corner stood a large box, a part of the building itself: it was eight feet high and open at the top, and it had been constructed as a sawdust magazine from which was drawn material for the horse's bed in a stall on the other side of the partition. The big box, so high and towerlike, so commodious, so suggestive, had ceased to fulfil its legitimate function; though, providentially, it had been at least half full of sawdust when the horse died. Two years had gone by since that passing; an interregnum in transportation during which Penrod's father was "thinking" (he explained sometimes) of an automobile. Meanwhile, the gifted and generous sawdust-box had served brilliantly in war and peace: it was Penrod's stronghold.

There was a partially defaced sign upon the front wall of the box; the donjon-keep had known mercantile impulses:

> *The O. K. RaBiT Co.*
> *PENROD ScHoFiELD AND CO.*
> *iNQuiRE FOR PRicEs*

This was a venture of the preceding vacation, and had netted, at one time, an accrued and owed profit of $1.38. Prospects had been brightest on the very eve of cataclysm. The storeroom was locked and guarded, but twenty-seven rabbits and Belgian hares, old and young, had perished here on a single night—through no

THE O.K. RABIT CO
PENROD SCHOFIELD AND CO
INQUIRE FOR PRICES

human agency, but in a foray of cats, the besiegers treacherously tunnelling up through the sawdust from the small aperture which opened into the stall beyond the partition. Commerce has its martyrs.

Penrod climbed upon a barrel, stood on tiptoe, grasped the rim of the box; then, using a knot-hole as a stirrup, threw one leg over the top, drew himself up, and dropped within. Standing upon the packed sawdust, he was just tall enough to see over the top.

Duke had not followed him into the storeroom, but remained near the open doorway in a concave and pessimistic attitude. Penrod felt in a dark corner of the box and laid hands upon a simple apparatus consisting of an old bushel-basket with a few yards of clothes-line tied to each of its handles. He passed the ends of the lines over a big spool, which revolved upon an axle of wire suspended from a beam overhead, and, with the aid of this improvised pulley, lowered the empty basket until it came to rest in an upright position upon the floor of the storeroom at the foot of the sawdust-box.

"Eleva-ter!" shouted Penrod. "Ting-ting!"

Duke, old and intelligently apprehensive, approached slowly, in a semicircular manner, deprecatingly, but with courtesy. He pawed the basket delicately; then, as if that were all his master had expected of him, uttered one bright bark, sat down, and looked up triumphantly. His hypocrisy was shallow: many a horrible quarter of an hour had taught him his duty in this matter.

"El-e-*vay*-ter!" shouted Penrod sternly. "You want me to come down there to you?"

Duke looked suddenly haggard. He pawed the basket feebly again and, upon another outburst from on high, prostrated himself flat. Again threatened, he gave a superb impersonation of a worm.

"You get in that el-e-*vay*-ter!"

Reckless with despair, Duke jumped into the basket, landing in a dishevelled posture, which he did not alter until he had been drawn up and poured out upon the floor of sawdust with the box. There, shuddering, he lay in doughnut shape and presently slumbered.

It was dark in the box, a condition that might have been remedied by sliding back a small wooden panel on runners, which would have let in ample light from the alley; but Penrod Schofield had more interesting means of illumination. He knelt, and from a former soap-box, in a corner, took a lantern, without a chimney, and a large oil-can, the leak in the latter being so nearly imperceptible that its banishment from household use had seemed to Penrod as inexplicable as it was providential.

He shook the lantern near his ear: nothing splashed; there was no sound but a dry clinking. But there was plenty of kerosene in the can; and he filled the lantern, striking a match to illumine the operation. Then he lit the lantern and hung it upon a nail against the wall. The sawdust floor was slightly impregnated with oil, and the open flame quivered in suggestive proximity to the side of the box;

however, some rather deep charrings of the plank against which the lantern hung offered evidence that the arrangement was by no means a new one, and indicated at least a possibility of no fatality occurring this time.

Next, Penrod turned up the surface of the sawdust in another corner of the floor, and drew forth a cigar-box in which were half a dozen cigarettes, made of hayseed and thick brown wrapping paper, a lead-pencil, an eraser, and a small note-book, the cover of which was labelled in his own handwriting:

"English Grammar. Penrod Schofield. Room 6, Ward School Nomber Seventh."

The first page of this book was purely academic; but the study of English undefiled terminated with a slight jar at the top of the second: "Nor must an adverb be used to modif——"

Immediately followed:

> "HARoLD RAMoREZ
> THE RoADAGENT
> OR WiLD LiFE AMoNG THE
> ROCKY MTS."

And the subsequent entries in the book appeared to have little concern with Room 6, Ward School Nomber Seventh.

CHAPTER 11
ROMANCE

THE AUTHOR OF "HAROLD RAMOREZ," etc., lit one of the hayseed cigarettes, seated himself comfortably, with his back against the wall and his right shoulder just under the lantern, elevated his knees to support the note-book, turned to a blank page, and wrote, slowly and earnestly:

"CHAPTER THE SIXTH"

He took a knife from his pocket, and, broodingly, his eyes upon the inward embryos of vision, sharpened his pencil. After that, he extended a foot and meditatively rubbed Duke's back with the side of his shoe. Creation, with Penrod, did not leap, full-armed, from the brain; but finally he began to produce. He wrote very slowly at first, and then with increasing rapidity; faster and faster, gathering momentum and growing more and more fevered as he sped, till at last the true fire came, without which no lamp of real literature may be made to burn.

Mr. Wilson reched for his gun but our hero had him covred and soon said Well I guess you don't come any of that on me my freind.

Well what makes you so sure about it sneered the other bitting his lip so savageley that the blood ran. You are nothing but a common Roadagent any way and I do not propose to be bafled by such, Ramorez laughed at this and kep Mr. Wilson covred by his ottomatick.

Soon the two men were struggling together in the death-roes but soon Mr Wilson got him bound and gaged his mouth and went away for awhile leavin our hero, it was dark and he writhd at his bonds writhing on the floor wile the rats came out of their holes and bit him and vernim got all over him from the floor of that helish spot but soon he managed to push the gag out of his mouth with the end of his toungeu and got all his bonds off.

Soon Mr Wilson came back to tant him with his helpless condition flowed by his gang of detectives and they said Oh look at Ramorez sneering at his plight and tanted him with his helpless condition because Ramorez had put the bonds back sos he would look the same but could throw them off him when he wanted to Just look at him now sneered they. To hear him talk you would thought he was hot stuff and they said Look at him now, him that was going to do so much, Oh I would not like to be in his fix.

Soon Harold got mad at this and jumped up with blasing eyes throwin off his bonds like they were air Ha Ha sneered he I guess you better not talk so much next time. Soon there flowed another awful struggle and siezin his ottomatick back from Mr Wilson he shot two of the detectives through the heart Bing Bing went

the ottomatick and two more went to meet their Maker only two detectives left now and so he stabbed one and the scondrel went to meet his Maker for now our hero was fighting for his very life. It was dark in there now for night had falen and a terrible view met the eye Blood was just all over everything and the rats were eatin the dead men.

Soon our hero manged to get his back to the wall for he was fighting for his very life now and shot Mr Wilson through the abodmen Oh said Mr Wilson you—— —— —— (The dashes are Penrod's.)

Mr Wilson stagerd back vile oaths soilin his lips for he was in pain Why you—— ——you sneered he I will get you yet—— ——you Harold Ramorez

The remainin scondrel had an ax which he came near our heros head with but missed him and ramand stuck in the wall Our heros amunition was exhauscd what was he to do, the remanin scondrel would soon get his ax lose so our hero sprung forward and bit him till his teeth met in the flech for now our hero was fighting for his very life. At this the remanin scondrel also cursed and swore vile oaths. Oh sneered he—— —— ——you Harold Ramorez what did you bite me for Yes sneered Mr Wilson also and he has shot me in the abdomen too the——

Soon they were both cursin and reviln him together Why

you—— —— —— —— ——
sneered they what did you want
to injure us for——you Harold Ramorez you have not got
any sence and you think you are
so much but you are no better
than anybody else and you are
a—— —— —— —— —— ——

Soon our hero could stand this
no longer. If you could learn to act
like gentlmen said he I would not
do any more to you now and your
low vile exppresions have not got
any effect on me only to injure
your own self when you go to
meet your Maker Oh I guess you
have had enogh for one day and
I think you have learned a lesson
and will not soon atemp to beard
Harold Ramorez again so with a
tantig laugh he cooly lit a cigarrete
and takin the keys of the cell from
Mr Wilson poket went on out.

Soon Mr Wilson and the
wonded detective manged to bind
up their wonds and got up off
the floor—— ——it I will have
that dasstads life now sneered
they if we have to swing for
it—— —— —— ——him he
shall not eccape us again the low
down—— —— —— —— ——

CHAPITER SEVENTH

A mule train of heavily laden
burros laden with gold from the
mines was to be seen wondering
among the highest clifts and gorgs
of the Rocky Mts and a tall man
with a long silken mustash and
a cartigde belt could be heard
cursin vile oaths because he well
knew this was the lair of Harold
Ramorez Why—— —— ——
you you—— —— —— ——
mules you sneered he because the
poor mules were not able to go
any quicker —— you I will show
you Why—— —— —— ——
—— ——it sneered he his oaths
growing viler and viler I will whip
you—— —— —— —— ——
—— ——you sos you will not
be able to walk for a week——
——you you mean old—— ——
—— —— —— —— —— ——
——mules you

Scarcly had the vile words left
his lips when——

"PENROD!"

It was his mother's voice, calling
from the back porch.

Simultaneously, the noon whistles
began to blow, far and near; and the
romancer in the sawdust-box, sum-
moned prosaically from steep mountain passes above the clouds, paused
with stubby pencil halfway from lip
to knee. His eyes were shining: there
was a rapt sweetness in his gaze. As he
wrote, his burden had grown lighter;
thoughts of Mrs. Lora Rewbush had
almost left him; and in particular as
he recounted (even by the chaste dash)
the annoyed expressions of Mr. Wilson, the wounded detective, and the
silken moustached mule-driver, he
had felt mysteriously relieved concerning the Child Sir Lancelot. Altogether
he looked a better and a brighter boy.

"Pen-*rod!*"

The rapt look faded slowly. He
sighed, but moved not.

"Penrod! We're having lunch early just on your account, so you'll have plenty of time to be dressed for the pageant. Hurry!"

There was silence in Penrod's aerie.

"*Pen*-rod!"

Mrs. Schofields voice sounded nearer, indicating a threatened approach. Penrod bestirred himself: he blew out the lantern, and shouted plaintively:

"Well, ain't I coming fast's I can?"

"Do hurry," returned the voice, withdrawing; and the kitchen door could be heard to close.

Languidly, Penrod proceeded to set his house in order.

Replacing his manuscript and pencil in the cigar-box, he carefully buried the box in the sawdust, put the lantern and oil-can back in the soap-box, adjusted the elevator for the reception of Duke, and, in no uncertain tone, invited the devoted animal to enter.

Duke stretched himself amiably, affecting not to hear; and when this pretence became so obvious that even a dog could keep it up no longer, sat down in a corner, facing it, his back to his master, and his head perpendicular, nose upward, supported by the convergence of the two walls. This, from a dog, is the last word, the comble of the immutable. Penrod commanded, stormed, tried gentleness; persuaded with honeyed words and pictured rewards. Duke's eyes looked backward; otherwise he moved not. Time elapsed. Penrod stooped to flattery, finally to insincere caresses; then, losing patience spouted sudden threats.

Duke remained immovable, frozen fast to his great gesture of implacable despair.

A footstep sounded on the threshold of the store-room.

"Penrod, come down from that box this instant!"

"Ma'am?"

"Are you up in that sawdust-box again?" As Mrs. Schofield had just heard her son's voice issue from the box, and also, as she knew he was there anyhow, her question must have been put for oratorical purposes only. "Because if you are," she continued promptly, "I'm going to ask your papa not to let you play there any——"

Penrod's forehead, his eyes, the tops of his ears, and most of his hair, became visible to her at the top of the box. "I ain't 'playing!'" he said indignantly.

"Well, what *are* you doing?"

"Just coming down," he replied, in a grieved but patient tone.

"Then why don't you *come*?"

"I got Duke here. I got to get him *down*, haven't I? You don't suppose I want to leave a poor dog in here to starve, do you?"

"Well, hand him down over the side to me. Let me——"

"I'll get him down all right," said Penrod. "I got him up here, and I guess I can get him down!"

"Well then, *do* it!"

"I will if you'll let me alone. If you'll go on back to the house I promise to be there inside of two minutes. Honest!"

He put extreme urgency into this, and his mother turned toward the house. "If you're not there in two minutes——"

"I will be!"

After her departure, Penrod expended some finalities of eloquence upon Duke, then disgustedly gathered him up in his arms, dumped him into the basket and, shouting sternly, "All in for the ground floor—step back there, madam—all ready, Jim!" lowered dog and basket to the floor of the storeroom. Duke sprang out in tumultuous relief, and bestowed frantic affection upon his master as the latter slid down from the box.

Penrod dusted himself sketchily, experiencing a sense of satisfaction, dulled by the overhanging afternoon, perhaps, but perceptible: he had the feeling of one who has been true to a cause. The operation of the elevator was unsinful and, save for the shock to Duke's nervous system, it was harmless; but Penrod could not possibly have brought himself to exhibit it in the presence of his mother or any other grown person in the world. The reasons for secrecy were undefined; at least, Penrod did not define them.

CHAPTER III
THE COSTUME

AFTER LUNCH HIS MOTHER AND HIS sister Margaret, a pretty girl of nineteen, dressed him for the sacrifice. They stood him near his mother's bedroom window and did what they would to him.

During the earlier anguishes of the process he was mute, exceeding the pathos of the stricken calf in the shambles; but a student of eyes might have perceived in his soul the premonitory symptoms of a sinister uprising. At a rehearsal (in citizens' clothes) attended by mothers and grown-up sisters, Mrs. Lora Rewbush had announced that she wished the costuming to be "as medieval and artistic as possible." Otherwise, and as to details, she said, she would leave the costumes entirely to the good taste of the children's parents. Mrs. Schofield and Margaret were no archeologists, but they knew that their taste was as good as that of other mothers and sisters concerned; so with perfect confidence they had planned and executed a costume for Penrod; and the only misgiving they felt was connected with the tractability of the Child Sir Lancelot himself.

Stripped to his underwear, he had been made to wash himself vehemently; then they began by shrouding his legs in a pair of silk stockings, once blue but now mostly whitish. Upon Penrod they visibly surpassed mere ampleness; but they were long, and it required only a rather loose imagination to assume that they were tights.

The upper part of his body was next concealed from view by a garment so peculiar that its description becomes difficult. In 1886, Mrs. Schofield, then unmarried, had worn at her "coming-out party" a dress of vivid salmon silk which had been remodelled after her marriage to accord with various epochs of fashion until a final, unskilful campaign at a dye-house had left it in a condition certain to attract much attention to the wearer. Mrs. Schofield had considered giving it to

Della, the cook; but had decided not to do so, because you never could tell how Della was going to take things, and cooks were scarce.

It may have been the word "medieval" (in Mrs. Lora Rewbush's rich phrase) which had inspired the idea for a last conspicuous usefulness; at all events, the bodice of that once salmon dress, somewhat modified and moderated, now took a position, for its farewell appearance in society, upon the back, breast, and arms of the Child Sir Lancelot.

The area thus costumed ceased at the waist, leaving a Jaeger-like and unmedieval gap thence to the tops of the stockings. The inventive genius of woman triumphantly bridged it, but in a manner which imposes upon history almost insuperable delicacies of narration. Penrod's father was an old-fashioned man: the twentieth century had failed to shake his faith in red flannel for cold weather; and it was while Mrs. Schofield was putting away her husband's winter underwear that she perceived how hopelessly one of the elder specimens had dwindled; and simultaneously she received the inspiration which resulted in a pair of trunks for the Child Sir Lancelot, and added an earnest bit of colour, as well as a genuine touch of the Middle Ages, to his costume. Reversed, fore to aft, with the greater part of the legs cut off, and strips of silver braid covering the seams, this garment, she felt, was not traceable to its original source.

When it had been placed upon Penrod, the stockings were attached to it by a system of safety-pins, not very perceptible at a distance. Next, after being severely warned against stooping, Penrod got his feet into the slippers he wore to dancing-school— "patent-leather pumps" now decorated with large pink rosettes.

"If I can't stoop," he began, smolderingly, "I'd like to know how'm I goin' to kneel in the pag——"

"You must *manage*!" This, uttered through pins, was evidently thought to be sufficient.

They fastened some ruching about his slender neck, pinned ribbons at random all over him, and then Margaret thickly powdered his hair.

"Oh, yes, that's all right," she said, replying to a question put by her mother. "They always powdered their hair in Colonial times."

"It doesn't seem right to me—exactly," objected Mrs. Schofield, gently. "Sir Lancelot must have been ever so long before Colonial times."

"That doesn't matter," Margaret reassured her. "Nobody'll know the difference—Mrs. Lora Rewbush least of all. I don't think she knows a thing about it, though, of course, she does write splendidly and the words of the pageant are just beautiful. Stand still, Penrod!" (The author of "Harold Ramorez" had moved convulsively.) "Besides, powdered hair's always becoming. Look at him. You'd hardly know it was Penrod!"

The pride and admiration with which she pronounced this undeniable truth might have been thought tactless, but Penrod, not analytical, found his spirits somewhat elevated. No mirror was in his range of vision and, though he had submitted to cursory

measurements of his person a week earlier, he had no previous acquaintance with the costume. He began to form a not unpleasing mental picture of his appearance, something somewhere between the portraits of George Washington and a vivid memory of Miss Julia Marlowe at a matinee of "Twelfth Night."

He was additionally cheered by a sword which had been borrowed from a neighbor, who was a Knight of Pythias. Finally there was a mantle, an old golf cape of Margaret's. Fluffy polka-dots of white cotton had been sewed to it generously; also it was ornamented with a large cross of red flannel, suggested by the picture of a Crusader in a newspaper advertisement. The mantle was fastened to Penrod's shoulder (that is, to the shoulder of Mrs. Schofield's ex-bodice) by means of large safety-pins, and arranged to hang down behind him, touching his heels, but obscuring nowise the glory of his facade. Then, at last, he was allowed to step before a mirror.

It was a full-length glass, and the worst immediately happened. It might have been a little less violent, perhaps, if Penrod's expectations had not been so richly and poetically idealized; but as things were, the revolt was volcanic.

Victor Hugo's account of the fight with the devil-fish, in "Toilers of the Sea," encourages a belief that, had Hugo lived and increased in power, he might have been equal to a proper recital of the half hour which followed Penrod's first sight of himself as the Child Sir Lancelot. But Mr. Wilson himself, dastard but eloquent foe of Harold Ramorez, could not have expressed, with all the vile dashes at his command, the sentiments which animated Penrod's bosom when the instantaneous and unalterable conviction descended upon him that he was intended by his loved ones to make a public spectacle of himself in his sister's stockings and part of an old dress of his mother's.

To him these familiar things were not disguised at all; there seemed no possibility that the whole world would not know them at a glance. The stockings were worse than the bodice. He had been assured that these could not be recognized, but, seeing them in the mirror, he was sure that no human eye could fail at first glance to detect the difference between himself and the former purposes of these stockings. Fold, wrinkle, and void shrieked their history with a hundred tongues, invoking earthquake, eclipse, and blue ruin. The frantic youth's final submission was obtained only after a painful telephonic conversation between himself and his father, the latter having been called up and upon, by the exhausted Mrs. Schofield, to subjugate his offspring by wire.

The two ladies made all possible haste, after this, to deliver Penrod into the hands of Mrs. Lora Rewbush; nevertheless, they found opportunity to exchange earnest congratulations upon his not having recognized the humble but serviceable paternal garment now brilliant about the Lancelotish middle. Altogether, they felt that the costume was a success. Penrod looked like nothing ever remotely imagined by Sir Thomas Malory or Alfred Tennyson;—for that matter, he looked like nothing ever before seen on earth; but as Mrs. Schofield and Margaret took their places in the audience at the Women's Arts and Guild Hall, the anxiety they felt concerning Penrod's elocutionary and gesticular powers, so soon to be put to public test, was pleasantly tempered by their satisfaction that, owing to their efforts, his outward appearance would be a credit to the family.

CHAPTER IV
DESPERATION

THE CHILD SIR LANCELOT FOUND himself in a large anteroom behind the stage—a room crowded with excited children, all about equally medieval and artistic. Penrod was less conspicuous than he thought himself, but he was so preoccupied with his own shame, steeling his nerves to meet the first inevitable taunting reference to his sister's stockings, that he failed to perceive there were others present in much of his own unmanned condition. Retiring to a corner, immediately upon his entrance, he managed to unfasten the mantle at the shoulders, and, drawing it round him, pinned it again at his throat so that it concealed the rest of his costume. This permitted a temporary relief, but increased his horror of the moment when, in pursuance of the action of the "pageant," the sheltering garment must be cast aside.

Some of the other child knights were also keeping their mantles close about them. A few of the envied opulent swung brilliant fabrics from their shoulders, airily, showing off hired splendours from a professional costumer's stock, while one or two were insulting examples of parental indulgence, particularly little Maurice Levy, the Child Sir Galahad. This shrinking person went clamorously about, making it known everywhere that the best tailor in town had been dazzled by a great sum into constructing his costume. It consisted of blue velvet knickerbockers, a white satin waistcoat, and a beautifully cut little swallow-tailed coat with pearl buttons. The medieval and artistic triumph was completed by a mantle of yellow velvet, and little white boots, sporting gold tassels.

All this radiance paused in a brilliant career and addressed the Child Sir Lancelot, gathering an immediately formed semicircular audience of little girls. Woman was ever the trailer of magnificence.

"What *you* got on?" inquired Mr. Levy, after dispensing information. "What you got on under that ole golf cape?"

Penrod looked upon him coldly. At other times his questioner would have approached him with deference, even with apprehension. But to-day the Child Sir Galahad was somewhat intoxicated with the power of his own beauty.

"What *you* got on?" he repeated.

"Oh, nothin'," said Penrod, with an indifference assumed at great cost to his nervous system.

The elate Maurice was inspired to set up as a wit. "Then you're nakid!" he shouted exultantly. "Penrod Schofield

says he hasn't got nothin' on under that ole golf cape! He's nakid! He's nakid."

The indelicate little girls giggled delightedly, and a javelin pierced the inwards of Penrod when he saw that the Child Elaine, amber-curled and beautiful Marjorie Jones, lifted golden laughter to the horrid jest.

Other boys and girls came flocking to the uproar. "He's nakid, he's nakid!" shrieked the Child Sir Galahad. "Penrod Schofield's nakid! He's *na-a-a-kid!*"

"Hush, hush!" said Mrs. Lora Rewbush, pushing her way into the group. "Remember, we are all little knights and ladies to-day. Little knights and ladies of the Table Round would not make so much noise. Now children, we must begin to take our places on the stage. Is everybody here?"

Penrod made his escape under cover of this diversion: he slid behind Mrs. Lora Rewbush, and being near a door, opened it unnoticed and went out quickly, closing it behind him. He found himself in a narrow and vacant hallway which led to a door marked "Janitor's Room."

Burning with outrage, heart-sick at the sweet, cold-blooded laughter of Marjorie Jones, Penrod rested his elbows upon a window-sill and speculated upon the effects of a leap from the second story. One of the reasons he gave it up was his desire to live on Maurice Levy's account: already he was forming educational plans for the Child Sir Galahad.

A stout man in blue overalls passed through the hallway muttering to himself petulantly. "I reckon they'll find that hall hot enough *now!*" he said, conveying to Penrod an impression that some too feminine women had sent him upon an unreasonable errand to the furnace. He went into the Janitor's Room and, emerging a moment later, minus the overalls, passed Penrod again with a bass rumble—"Dern ,em!" it seemed he said—and made a gloomy exit by the door at the upper end of the hallway.

The conglomerate and delicate rustle of a large, mannerly audience was heard as the janitor opened and closed the door; and stage-fright seized the boy. The orchestra began an overture, and, at that, Penrod, trembling violently, tiptoed down the hall into the Janitor's Room. It was a cul-de-sac: There was no outlet save by the way he had come.

Despairingly he doffed his mantle and looked down upon himself for a last sickening assurance that the stockings were as obviously and disgracefully Margaret's as they had seemed in the mirror at home. For a moment he was encouraged: perhaps he was no worse than some of the other boys. Then he noticed that a safety-pin had opened; one of those connecting the stockings with his trunks. He sat down to fasten it and his eye fell for the first time with particular attention upon the trunks. Until this instant he had been preoccupied with the stockings.

Slowly recognition dawned in his eyes.

The Schofields' house stood on a corner at the intersection of two main-travelled streets; the fence was low, and the publicity obtained by the washable portion of the family apparel, on Mondays, had often been painful to Penrod; for boys have a peculiar sensitiveness in these matters. A plain, matter-of-fact washerwoman' employed by Mrs. Schofield, never left anything to the imagination of the passer-by; and of all her calm display the scarlet flaunting of his father's winter wear had most abashed Penrod. One day Marjorie Jones, all gold and starch, had passed when the dreadful things were on the line: Penrod had hidden himself, shuddering. The whole town, he was convinced, knew these garments intimately and derisively.

And now, as he sat in the janitor's chair, the horrible and paralyzing recognition came. He had not an instant's doubt that every fellow actor, as well as every soul in the audience, would recognize what his mother and sister had put upon him. For as the awful truth became plain to himself it seemed blazoned to the world; and far, far louder than the stockings, the trunks did fairly bellow the grisly secret: *whose* they were and *what* they were!

Most people have suffered in a dream the experience of finding themselves very inadequately clad in the midst of a crowd of well-dressed people, and such dreamers' sensations are comparable to Penrod's, though faintly, because Penrod was awake and in much too full possession of the most active capacities for anguish.

A human male whose dress has been damaged, or reveals some vital lack, suffers from a hideous and shameful loneliness which makes every second absolutely unbearable until he is again as others of his sex and species; and there is no act or sin whatever too desperate for him in his struggle to attain that condition. Also, there is absolutely no embarrassment possible to a woman which is comparable to that of a man under corresponding circumstances and in this a boy is a man. Gazing upon the ghastly trunks, the stricken Penrod felt that he was a degree worse then nude; and a great horror of himself filled his soul.

"Penrod Schofield!"

The door into the hallway opened, and a voice demanded him. He could not be seen from the hallway, but the hue and the cry was up; and he knew he must be taken. It was only a question of seconds. He huddled in his chair.

"Penrod Schofield!" cried Mrs. Lora Rewbush angrily.

The distracted boy rose and, as he did so, a long pin sank deep into his back. He extracted it frenziedly, which brought to his ears a protracted and sonorous ripping, too easily located by a final gesture of horror.

"Penrod Schofield!" Mrs. Lora Rewbush had come out into the hallway.

And now, in this extremity, when all seemed lost indeed, particularly including honour, the dilating eye of the outlaw fell upon the blue overalls which the janitor had left hanging upon a peg.

Inspiration and action were almost simultaneous.

CHAPTER V
THE PAGEANT OF THE TABLE ROUND

"PENROD!" MRS. LORA REWBUSH stood in the doorway, indignantly gazing upon a Child Sir Lancelot mantled to the heels. "Do you know that you have kept an audience of five hundred people waiting for ten minutes?" She,

also, detained the five hundred while she spake further.

"Well," said Penrod contentedly, as he followed her toward the buzzing stage, "I was just sitting there thinking."

Two minutes later the curtain rose on a medieval castle hall richly done in the new stage-craft made in Germany and consisting of pink and blue cheesecloth. The Child King Arthur and the Child Queen Guinevere were disclosed upon thrones, with the Child Elaine and many other celebrities in attendance; while about fifteen Child Knights were seated at a dining-room table round, which was covered with a large Oriental rug, and displayed (for the knights' refreshment) a banquet service of silver loving-cups and trophies, borrowed from the Country Club and some local automobile manufacturers.

In addition to this splendour, potted plants and palms have seldom been more lavishly used in any castle on the stage or off.

The footlights were aided by a "spot-light" from the rear of the hall; and the children were revealed in a blaze of glory.

A hushed, multitudinous "O-OH" of admiration came from the decorous and delighted audience. Then the children sang feebly:

> *"Chuldrun of the Tabul Round,*
> *Lit-tul knights and ladies we.*
> *Let our voy-siz all resound*
> *Faith and hope and charitee!"*

The Child King Arthur rose, extended his sceptre with the decisive gesture of a semaphore, and spake:

"Each littul knight and lady born
Has noble deeds to perform
In thee child-world of shivullree,
No matter how small his share may be.
Let each advance and tell in turn
What claim has each to knighthood earn."

The Child Sir Mordred, the villain of this piece, rose in his place at the table round, and piped the only lines ever written by Mrs. Lora Rewbush which Penrod Schofield could have pronounced without loathing. Georgie Bassett, a really angelic boy, had been selected for the role of Mordred. His perfect conduct had earned for him the sardonic sobriquet, "The Little Gentleman," among his boy acquaintances. (Naturally he had no friends.) Hence the other boys supposed that he had been selected for the wicked Mordred as a reward of virtue. He declaimed serenely:

"I hight Sir Mordred the Child, and I teach
Lessons of selfishest evil, and reach
Out into darkness. Thoughtless, unkind,
And ruthless is Mordred, and unrefined."

The Child Mordred was properly rebuked and denied the accolade, though, like the others, he seemed to have assumed the title already. He made a plotter's exit. Whereupon Maurice Levy rose, bowed, announced that he highted the Child Sir Galahad, and continued with perfect sang-froid:

"I am the purest of the pure.
I have but kindest thoughts each day.

I give my riches to the poor,
And follow in the Master's way."

This elicited tokens of approval from the Child King Arthur, and he bade Maurice "stand forth" and come near the throne, a command obeyed with the easy grace of conscious merit.

It was Penrod's turn. He stepped back from his chair, the table between him and the audience, and began in a high, breathless monotone:

"I hight Sir Lancelot du Lake, the Child,
Gentul-hearted, meek, and mild.
What though I'm but a littul child,
Gentul-heartud, meek, and mild,
I do my share though but—though
but——"

Penrod paused and gulped. The voice of
Mrs. Lora Rewbush was heard from the
wings, prompting irritably, and the Child.
Sir Lancelot repeated:
"I do my share though but—though but a tot,
I pray you knight Sir Lancelot!"

This also met the royal favour, and Penrod was bidden to join Sir Galahad at the throne. As he crossed the stage, Mrs. Schofield whispered to Margaret:

"That boy! He's unpinned his mantle and fixed it to cover his whole costume. After we worked so hard to make it becoming!"

"Never mind; he'll have to take the cape off in a minute," returned Margaret. She leaned forward suddenly, narrowing her eyes to see better. "What *is* that thing hanging about his left ankle?" she whispered uneasily. "How queer! He must have got tangled in something."

"Where?" asked Mrs. Schofield, in alarm.

"His left foot. It makes him stumble. Don't you see? It looks—it looks like an elephant's foot!"

The Child Sir Lancelot and the Child Sir Galahad clasped hands before their Child King. Penrod was conscious of a great uplift; in a moment he would have to throw aside his mantle, but even so he was protected and sheltered in the human garment of a man. His stage-fright had passed, for the audience was but an indistinguishable blur of darkness beyond the dazzling lights. His most repulsive speech (that in which he proclaimed himself a "tot") was over and done with; and now at last the small, moist hand of the Child Sir Galahad lay within his own. Craftily his brown fingers stole from Maurice's palm to the wrist. The two boys declaimed in concert:

"We are two chuldrun of the Tabul Round
Strewing kindness all a-round.
With love and good deeds striving ever for the best,
May our littul efforts e'er be blest.
Two littul hearts we offer. See
United in love, faith, hope, and char—
OW!"

The conclusion of the duet was marred. The Child Sir Galahad suddenly stiffened, and, uttering an irrepressible shriek of anguish, gave a brief exhibition of the contortionist's art. ("HE'S TWISTIN' MY WRIST! DERN YOU, LEGGO!")

The voice of Mrs. Lora Rewbush was again heard from the wings; it sounded bloodthirsty. Penrod released his victim; and the Child King Arthur, somewhat disconcerted, extended his sceptre and, with the assistance of the enraged prompter, said:

"Sweet child-friends of the Tabul Round,
In brotherly love and kindness abound,
Sir Lancelot, you have spoken well,
Sir Galahad, too, as clear as bell.
So now pray doff your mantles gay.
You shall be knighted this very day."

And Penrod doffed his mantle.

Simultaneously, a thick and vasty gasp came from the audience, as from five hundred bathers in a wholly unexpected surf. This gasp was punctuated irregularly, over the auditorium, by imperfectly subdued screams both of dismay and incredulous joy, and by two dismal shrieks. Altogether it was an extraordinary sound, a sound never to be forgotten by any one who heard it. It was almost as unforgettable as the sight which caused it; the word "sight" being here used in its vernacular sense, for Penrod, standing unmantled and revealed in all the medieval and artistic glory of the janitor's blue overalls, falls within its meaning.

The janitor was a heavy man, and his overalls, upon Penrod, were merely oceanic. The boy was at once swaddled and lost within their blue gulfs and vast saggings; and the left leg, too hastily rolled up, had descended with a distinctively elephantine effect, as Margaret had observed. Certainly, the Child Sir Lancelot was at least a sight.

It is probable that a great many in that hall must have had, even then, a consciousness that they were looking on at History in the Making. A supreme act is recognizable at sight: it bears the birthmark of immortality. But Penrod, that marvellous boy, had begun to declaim, even with the gesture of flinging off his mantle for the accolade:

"I first, the Child Sir Lancelot du Lake,
Will volunteer to knighthood take,
And kneeling here before your throne
I vow to——"

He finished his speech unheard. The audience had recovered breath, but had lost self-control, and there ensued something later described by a participant as a sort of cultured riot.

The actors in the "pageant" were not so dumfounded by Penrod's costume as might have been expected. A few precocious geniuses perceived that the overalls were the Child Lancelot's own comment on maternal intentions; and these were profoundly impressed: they regarded him with the grisly admiration of young and ambitious criminals for a jail-mate about to be distinguished by hanging. But most of the children simply took it to be the case (a little strange, but not startling) that Penrod's mother had dressed him like that—which is pathetic. They tried to go on with the "pageant."

They made a brief, manful effort. But the irrepressible outbursts from the audience bewildered them; every time Sir Lancelot du Lake the Child opened his mouth, the great, shadowy house fell into an uproar, and the children into confusion. Strong women and brave girls in the audience went out into the lobby, shrieking and clinging to one another. Others remained, rocking in their seats, helpless and spent. The neighbourhood of Mrs. Schofield and Margaret became,

tactfully, a desert. Friends of the author went behind the scenes and encountered a hitherto unknown phase of Mrs. Lora Rewbush; they said, afterward, that she hardly seemed to know what she was doing. She begged to be left alone somewhere with Penrod Schofield, for just a little while.

They led her away.

CHAPTER VI
EVENING

THE SUN WAS SETTING BEHIND THE back fence (though at a considerable distance) as Penrod Schofield approached that fence and looked thoughtfully up at the top of it, apparently having in mind some purpose to climb up and sit there. Debating this, he passed his fingers gently up and down the backs of his legs; and then something seemed to decide him not to sit anywhere. He leaned against the fence, sighed profoundly, and gazed at Duke, his wistful dog.

The sigh was reminiscent: episodes of simple pathos were passing before his inward eye. About the most painful was the vision of lovely Marjorie Jones, weeping with rage as the Child Sir Lancelot was dragged, insatiate, from the prostrate and howling Child Sir Galahad, after an onslaught delivered the precise instant the curtain began to fall upon the demoralized "pageant." And then—oh, pangs! oh, woman!—she slapped at the ruffian's cheek, as he was led past her by a resentful janitor; and turning, flung

her arms round the Child Sir Galahad's neck.

"PENROD SCHOFIELD, DON'T
YOU DARE EVER SPEAK TO ME
AGAIN AS LONG AS YOU LIVE!"
Maurice's little white boots and gold
tassels had done their work.

At home the late Child Sir
Lancelot was consigned to a locked
clothes-closet pending the arrival of
his father. Mr. Schofield came and,
shortly after, there was put into practice an old patriarchal custom. It is a
custom of inconceivable antiquity:
probably primordial, certainly pre-
historic, but still in vogue in some
remaining citadels of the ancient sim-
plicities of the Republic.

And now, therefore, in the dusk,
Penrod leaned against the fence and
sighed.

His case is comparable to that of
an adult who could have survived a
similar experience. Looking back to
the sawdust-box, fancy pictures this
comparable adult a serious and inventive writer engaged in congenial literary activities in a private retreat. We
see this period marked by the creation
of some of the most virile passages of
a Work dealing exclusively in red cor-
puscles and huge primal impulses. We
see this thoughtful man dragged from
his calm seclusion to a horrifying publicity; forced to adopt the stage and,
himself a writer, compelled to exploit
the repulsive sentiments of an author
not only personally distasteful to him
but whose whole method and school
in belles lettres he despises.

We see him reduced by desper-
ation and modesty to stealing a pair
of overalls. We conceive him to have

ruined, then, his own reputation, and
to have utterly disgraced his family;
next, to have engaged in the duello and
to have been spurned by his lady-love,
thus lost to him (according to her own
declaration) forever. Finally, we must
behold: imprisonment by the author-
ities; the third degree and flagellation.

We conceive our man decided that
his career had been perhaps too event-
ful. Yet Penrod had condensed all of it
into eight hours.

It appears that he had at least some
shadowy perception of a recent fulness
of life, for, as he leaned against the
fence, gazing upon his wistful Duke,
he sighed again and murmured aloud:

"WELL, HASN'T THIS BEEN
A DAY!"

But in a little while a star came
out, freshly lighted, from the highest
part of the sky, and Penrod, looking
up, noticed it casually and a little
drowsily. He yawned. Then he sighed
once more, but not reminiscently:
evening had come; the day was over. It
was a sigh of pure ennui.

TO BE CONTINUED IN LITERARY OUTLAW #3

CONTRIBUTORS

PHILIP K. DICK (1928 – 1982) was an American science fiction writer and novelist. He wrote 44 novels and about 121 short stories, most of which appeared in science fiction magazines during his lifetime.

GARDNER FOX (1911 – 1986) was an American writer known best for creating numerous comic book characters for DC Comics. He is estimated to have written more than 4,000 comics stories,[4] including 1,500 for DC Comics. Fox was also a science fiction author and wrote many novels and short stories.

H. P. LOVECRAFT (1890 – 1937) was an American writer of weird, science, fantasy, and horror fiction. He is best known for his creation of the Cthulhu Mythos.

KEVIN G. SUMMERS is the author of *Legendarium, The Man Who Shot John Wilkes Booth*, and *The Bleak December*.

PATTY SUMMERS (1947 – 2012) lived in Stratford, New Hampshire. She was the editor of the literary magazine, *Phoebe*, and wrote several novels, including *Sugarloaf* and *The Brunswick Journals*.

BOOTH TARKINGTON (1869 – 1946) was an American novelist and dramatist best known for his novels The Magnificent Ambersons (1918) and Alice Adams (1921). He is one of only four novelists to win the Pulitzer Prize for Fiction more than once.

THORNTON WILDER (1897 – 1975) was an American playwright and novelist. He won three Pulitzer Prizes for the novel *The Bridge of San Luis Rey* and for the plays *Our Town* and *The Skin of Our Teeth*.